Something About Aimee

S.E. SMITH

Acknowledgments

I would like to thank my husband, Steve, for believing in me and being proud enough of me to give me the courage to follow my dream. I would also like to give a special thank you to my sister and best friend, Linda, who not only encouraged me to write, but who also read the manuscript. Also, to my other friends who believe in me: Julie, Jackie, Christel, Sally, Jolanda, Lisa, Laurelle, Debbie, and Narelle. The girls that keep me going!

And a special thanks to Paul Heitsch, David Brenin, Samantha Cook, Suzanne Elise Freeman, PJ Ochlan, Vincent Fallow, L. Sophie Helbig, and Hope Newhouse—the outstanding voices behind my audiobooks!

– S. E. Smith

Contemporary Romance
SOMETHING ABOUT AIMEE:
GIRLS FROM THE STREET BOOK 1
Copyright © 2022 by S.E. Smith
First E-Book Published June 2022
Cover Design by Melody Simmons

ALL RIGHTS RESERVED: This literary work may not be reproduced or transmitted in any form or by any means, including electronic or photographic reproduction, in whole or in part, without express written permission from the author.

All characters, places, and events in this book are fictitious or have been used fictitiously, and are not to be construed as real. Any resemblance to actual persons living or dead, actual events, locales, or organizations are strictly coincidental.

Summary: A Royal Sheikh's life is turned upside down when he falls in love with the street-smart courier who saves his life.

ISBN: 9781956052602 (Paperback)
ISBN: 9781956052596 (eBook)

Romance (love, explicit sexual content) | Contemporary | Action/Adventure

Published by Montana Publishing, LLC
& SE Smith of Florida Inc. www.sesmithfl.com

Contents

Chapter 1	1
Chapter 2	9
Chapter 3	17
Chapter 4	28
Chapter 5	38
Chapter 6	45
Chapter 7	51
Chapter 8	60
Chapter 9	71
Chapter 10	81
Chapter 11	89
Chapter 12	96
Chapter 13	103
Chapter 14	114
Chapter 15	120
Chapter 16	126
Chapter 17	133
Chapter 18	143
Chapter 19	153
Chapter 20	159
Chapter 21	165
Chapter 22	175
Epilogue	183
Additional Books	191
About the Author	195

Synopsis

She was born on the streets; he was born to rule...

Aimee Wheels loves her free-living lifestyle. She doesn't need the trappings of money to find happiness. All she needs are her crazy friends, her job as a courier in New York City, and her skateboard.

Sheikh Qadir Saif-Ad-Din understands the power behind money and royalty, and he knows how to wield it. When he is simultaneously dismissed and then saved by a woman in tattered jeans carrying a skateboard, he doesn't know what to think—except that he wants her!

Aimee is thrown into the world of the ultra-rich when she stops an assassination attempt against Qadir, and it doesn't take much for her to become a target herself. It's possible to rise above the dangers like a phoenix, but time and distrust can ruin even the best of relationships, and Aimee and Qadir have led very different lives. Can love find a way despite a rival billionaire trying to kill them?

A USA Today and NY Times bestselling author, the internationally acclaimed S.E. Smith presents a new story with her signature humor and unpredictable twists! Exciting adventure, hot romance, and iconic characters have won her a legion of fans. More than TWO MILLION books sold!

One

"Listen up!" Stanley Becker yelled, his deep baritone voice booming in the small space. "I need a volunteer to deliver a letter downtown."

In the crowded workroom of Becker Courier Services in Upper East Manhattan, a chorus of groans greeted his announcement. Stanley's gaze swept over the six occupants of the room, and each person looked the other way when he focused on them as if that would make them invisible.

The room was organized chaos. Bicycles, some intact and ready to go, others in pieces with greasy parts scattered on old envelopes and newspapers, jockeyed for space with the dilapidated loveseat, banged up desks, and lockers.

Couriers of all different shapes, sizes, and colors fought for the limited seating as they finished their last-minute paperwork before quitting time or choked down the fast food that they had grabbed after not eating all day.

When no one responded, Stanley yelled, "Carl!"

"Can't do it, boss," Carl shouted back. "Taxi driver on 57th bent my rim."

Stanley's curse-riddled opinion on taxi drivers caused snickers to abound.

"Eric," Stanley barked.

Eric was already shaking his head. "Can't, boss. I've already got over forty hours this week, and tonight's dinner with my future in-laws. Becky said if I was late, that was it."

Polly held up her hands. "I'm out. I've got a flight in two hours and Shu promised to drive me, so don't bother asking her. I'll be lucky to make it to the airport as it is."

Stanley slammed his hand on the counter and scowled. "This has to be at the Harris building by 6 p.m.!"

Everyone's eyes went to the large atomic clock on the wall. Trace scoffed and shook his head. Carl snorted and continued working on his bike.

"It's 5:30 on a Friday night, boss," Carl replied. "No one can make that run and get it there by 6 p.m. It's impossible."

"What's impossible?"

Everyone's eyes turned from Carl to the owner of the new voice.

Aimee Wheels stepped on the back of her skateboard and caught it in midair. A courier bag was draped across her body. She reached into her pocket, retrieved a brand new bike tube, and tossed it to Carl. Aimee had witnessed his collision and picked up the replacement piece on the way back from her last delivery.

As Aimee tucked her board under her arm, threaded her way through the cluttered room, and dropped the receipts for her deliveries on the long, scarred counter in front of Stanley, he replied, "A rush job came in. Company paid top dollar to have this delivered at the Harris building to some foreign guy, but it has to be there by 6 p.m."

Aimee whistled under her breath and shook her head. "Sounds like the guy who dropped it off should have planned better." She signed the log.

"I bet Wheels could make it," Eric called with a mischievous look in his eyes.

"Twenty says she can't," Peter countered.

"Ten says she can," Polly said, stuffing an Alexander Hamilton in the betting jar on the counter.

Aimee was already shaking her head. If she had left five minutes ago, she might have made it. The Harris building was all the way down near the Financial district and the traffic was crazy at this hour.

Carl stood up and added another twenty to the pot. Aimee groaned.

"Two-hundred-dollar bonus if you deliver on time."

Everyone froze, including Aimee. She looked at Stanley, then the clock, and finally the folder Stanley held out to her.

Two hundred dollars was a lot! Stanley never offered more than a ten-dollar bonus on special deliveries. Between the bonus and her share of the winnings if she made it in time, she would have a nice little cushion for a few weeks.

The silence was broken when Polly softly chanted, "Wheels… Wheels… Wheels…"

Aimee bit her lip, then grabbed the envelope and stuffed it in her courier bag. She turned and took off at a sprint, jumping over the loveseat with one hand and tossing her skateboard with the other. Her feet hit the board, and she grabbed the frame of the door as she made a sharp turn into the lobby. In no time at all, she had left the building with incredible speed.

"Damn, I think she might just make it," Peter grumbled.

Aimee flew along the crowded roads. She hugged her board, keeping low so she could swerve in and out of traffic. She caught the back of a city bus on Madison Avenue, a police cruiser on East 23rd, and another one heading down Broadway before she caught an ambulance on Lafayette Street. She cut between the towering skyscrapers to Centre, taking alleys most people didn't even know existed.

She emerged out of an alley on Fulton Street near the Harris building with two minutes to spare. Kicking her board up, she caught it and sprinted to the revolving door, sliding in a narrow, closing gap as a crowd of workers made their way out. She pulled the letter out of her bag and tried to quiet her pounding heart as she walked up to the main reception desk.

"Delivery for Suite 1805." Aimee handed her courier badge to the receptionist and scanned the barcode on the envelope before she handed that to the woman as well.

The receptionist took the letter and passed it to a young man who was waiting. "I can't believe it made it on time," the man said with a relieved smile before he darted off to the elevators.

Aimee raised her eyebrow and ruefully shook her head. "Yeah, it just sprouted wings and flew through rush hour traffic. Thanks for the tip, dude," she muttered before she turned the scanner around in front of the receptionist with a smile. "Can you please sign this?"

The phone rang and the woman answered it. Aimee waited, but apparently the receptionist could not sign her name and talk at the same time. Aimee tapped her fingers on the counter. From the way the woman turned away and was giggling, the call wasn't business related.

Aimee pulled the pocket watch out of her ragged coat pocket and glanced at it. She looked up when a group of men entered the building. They were all dressed in nice black clothes, and they were wired.

It didn't take her long to assess the situation. The first two men who entered were the lookouts. Next came the head of security. Aimee wanted to roll her eyes. No doubt the next person would be the 'big guy', whoever that was.

She knew it would be a guy because women seldom made an entrance like this. Most of the high-society ladies preferred a less conspicuous entrance that didn't scream 'come kidnap me'.

Sure enough, the next man who entered was obviously the one being protected. Aimee looked him over, itemizing each article of clothing from his fifty-thousand-dollar suit to the high-priced shoes, gold and diamond cufflinks, and Piaget Polo watch on his wrist.

Hell, even his sunglasses cost more than I make in five years, she thought.

Polly's rubric would label him drop-dead gorgeous. Aimee had seen plenty of gorgeous guys who didn't have an ounce of humanity in their self-important bodies, so unless this one showed her something different, he would barely make it into the cute category of her own rating system.

When he removed his sunglasses, their eyes collided, and she felt a shiver of unease. His dark brown eyes conveyed a sudden, intense shock and then he intently looked her over from head to toe as if trying to ferret out all her secrets.

Aimee analyzed his features, but no, she was certain she had never seen him before. Maybe Mr. High and Mighty had never seen a poor person before. She snorted and didn't bother to hide her smirk.

Mr. Moneybags' expression was thunderous and Aimee almost laughed out loud. If he thought he could intimidate her, he was barking up the wrong tree. She had dealt with guys that would make this poor sod wet his bed.

She noticed the two bodyguards entering behind him and released a soft whistle. Five bodyguards would set him back a pretty penny. Her fingers itched to test how good they were before she pushed the thought away. She was done with that life.

That thought did make her laugh, and she shook her head. Who was she kidding? Never say never.

"Here you go," the receptionist said.

"Thanks. Have a great weekend." Aimee slid the scanner and badge into her courier bag, adjusted the skateboard under her arm, and turned to exit the building.

She had almost passed Mr. Top of the World when the revolving doors spun, and intense alarm shot through her system. Years of living in neighborhoods where drive-by shootings were as common as fast-food drive-throughs had conditioned her. Before the two men were all the way through the door, she saw the guns in their hands. Their eyes were still scanning the lobby, but she knew who their target would be.

"Take cover!" she hollered.

She dropped her skateboard, caught it with her foot, and sent it careening toward the two assailants just as she twisted and tackled Mr. Come Kidnap Me. Gunfire erupted and screams filled the lobby. A burning pain seared Aimee's arm, but she ignored it. They were sitting ducks in the lobby.

She rolled over the man. Their eyes connected again for a second. In his dark chocolate irises she saw understanding and calm. She gave him a brief nod in acknowledgment.

Shouts in Arabic gave her a clue about the man's nationality—or at least his bodyguards'. Over the din, she said, "Run when I tell you."

He lifted an eyebrow, but she was already twisting away—and discovered that her plan to distract the gunmen wouldn't be necessary. Her shout and skateboard missile had provided the bodyguards with enough warning to take care of the assailants.

But not without injuries, she thought when she saw blood staining a guard's pant leg.

"Qadir, this way," the chief of security ordered.

Mr. Calm in a Crisis—whose real name was 'Qadir' apparently—ignored his security guy and grabbed her arm. She whirled toward him and tried to pull free, but he tightened his hold.

"You got them. I've got to go," she said, looking at the door. She heard sirens. She tugged again to free herself.

"You'll come with me," he stated.

"Qadir, your hand. You're injured?" the head security guy exclaimed.

Aimee's captor frowned and looked down at his hand. Bright red blood oozed between his fingers. He shook his head, his eyes focused on her face.

"The blood is not mine," he said in a low voice that sent a shiver through her.

He relaxed his grip, and she hissed, wincing and reaching for her arm. He grimaced, and the look in his eyes made her wonder if perhaps she had been hasty about discounting his ability to last on the street.

"Tarek, call my physician," he ordered.

Aimee nodded with approval. "Your guy is going to need some help. The gunmen must not have hit an artery, otherwise he would've bled out by now."

The two bodyguards that had been in the rear were now standing over the two assailants. Neither gunman was moving, but the wounded bodyguard remained standing with his weapon trained on the neutralized threats.

"This doctor is for you," Qadir growled. "Nizar will be seen by someone else."

The protest on her lips died when Qadir ushered her into the elevator and suddenly she was surrounded by Tarek, the two forward bodyguards, and the man they were protecting. All four men made her feel like a shrimp.

She reminded herself that being five foot three and three quarters in her stocking feet tended to make everyone seem like a giant, but there was no doubt that their muscled height and breadth were excessive in this small space, especially Qadir's. She looked at the elevator display as the lift began to climb and silently groaned.

So much for enjoying a nice evening on the water with my friends tonight, she disgruntledly thought, wishing she could at least lean back against the side of the elevator.

"I need my board," she suddenly said.

Qadir frowned down at her. "Your board?"

She nodded. "My skateboard. I shoved it at the lunatics downstairs before they started shooting. I need it back."

The man relayed her request to his head of security in Arabic, and Aimee turned her head so he couldn't see the smile on her lips. She was fluent in a few languages. That tended to happen when you lived in a housing project which was a multicultural world unto itself.

"So, do people normally try to kill you on Friday nights, or is today a special day?" she asked.

Two

MINUTES BEFORE:

Sheik Qadir Saif-Ad-Din entered the limousine and tried to quell his irritation at being late for his last meeting of the evening.

His plans for an enjoyable, relaxing evening had been canceled. The meeting he was on his way to now had been planned for earlier, but it was rescheduled when the owner of the company had a heart attack.

"Mr. Carthmen signed the papers, and his son dropped them with a local courier service. The board of directors should receive them shortly," his brother, Tarek Saif-Ad-Din, reported.

"Did you inform them that if the documents are not there by the time that I arrive, the offer will be rescinded?"

Tarek bowed his head in acknowledgement. "Of course," he replied with an amused grin.

"I should have just let you handle this," Qadir mused.

Tarek's eyebrow raised. "You are in pursuit of a new mistress?" he sardonically asked.

"I was, but it has been delayed—again."

"You *should* have let me handle this," Tarek chuckled.

"The lovely Lydia St. Michaels would wholeheartedly agree."

"*The* Lydia St. Michaels? Is she even divorced from her fourth husband yet?" Tarek politely inquired.

Qadir frowned. "Third," he replied.

Tarek shook his head and held up four fingers. "Fourth. I'm not the Head of Intelligence for nothing. I *read* the reports that are given to me, especially those involving your… close associates."

Qadir's smile was sardonic. "As long as she is not expecting me to be husband number five, I could not care less if she is still married." He shrugged and looked at his wristwatch. "We are going to be late."

Tarek glanced out the window. "There are some things that even I can't control, and that includes Friday evening traffic in New York City. Still, I believe we will arrive at the building precisely at 6 p.m., and I don't believe the Board of Directors will be concerned if we are five minutes late."

They arrived at precisely six. Qadir didn't know why he had doubted his younger brother. Tarek's eye for detail was impeccable.

The two bodyguards in the black SUV ahead exited their vehicle. A moment later, the door to the limousine opened and Tarek stepped out, scanning the area before he stepped aside.

As Crown Prince and next ruler of the small but extremely wealthy Kingdom of Jawahir, Qadir normally *would* have let one of his three brothers handle this situation. His decision to oversee this acquisition had more to do with revenge than with necessity.

Andrew Carthmen thought he could get away with embezzling and selling trade information to a rival company. For that, Qadir would make this man sell his company for the amount of money already taken or go to prison.

Exiting the limousine, Qadir pulled a pair of sunglasses from his pocket and put them on for the short walk to the revolving doors.

Behind them, two bodyguards emerged from the SUV that had followed their limousine. They took up the rear.

A frigid burst of November wind swept between the buildings. For just a moment, the cold air reminded him of desert temperatures at night, until irritating honking sounds and the taint of petrol in the air dissipated the memory.

A wave of distaste filled him. He would much rather have an endless ocean of sand than these glass pillars. The wealth in his country went far beyond the rare gems and minerals required for the world's microchips. Jawahir was beautiful and wild in a way this claustrophobic maze could never touch.

Tarek's knowing look made him shake his head. His brother had a higher tolerance for the bustle of the city than he did. The only thing Qadir liked about the city was the beautiful women who preferred to live here. None of his mistresses had ever been to the desert. The sand would ruin their perfectly made-up faces, hair, and was hardly suitable for the six-inch heels they loved to wear—sometimes even in bed.

The forward guard entered the building first. Tarek and Qadir followed.

Qadir paused inside the lobby, scanning the area out of habit. Men and women in professional attire paused and stared when they saw him. Tarek stepped up next to him and grinned.

"You always could quiet a room with just an entrance, brother," Tarek mused.

"Jealous?" he teased.

He removed his sunglasses and paused as he registered one small figure who was completely out of place in the posh lobby. At first, he thought the person a ragtag boy, but then she looked up and violet eyes outlined in thick, black lashes locked with his. A tingling sensation swept through him and awareness hit him with the force of a blow. Blood rushed downward, and he was instantly hard.

"Qadir? Are you alright?" Tarek asked.

Tarek's voice was muted, only background noise. Qadir had heard of *Almukhtar*, the Chosen. It was said to be a myth, though his parents swore it was real. Neither he nor his three brothers had ever found *Almukhtar*. At thirty, he had believed that if there was such a connection to one woman, he would have already experienced it with one of the many women he had met around the world.

He hungrily studied the woman's petite figure. It was hard to tell much about her body. Besides the fact that the battered piece of wood she held was partially obstructing the view of her torso, she wore an oversized ragged coat, torn baggy denims, dirty running shoes—

He frowned and stared at her shoes. Was that duct tape on the toes? His gaze retraced the path from her tattered shoes, moving at a slow and sensual pace, mentally replacing her clothes with the finest silk, until he reached her face again.

Incredulous anger spread through him when he saw her mocking expression. She turned away from him as if he wasn't worth her time. He blinked. Never had he encountered a woman who would dismiss him with such impudence!

She spoke to the receptionist, flashed an easy smile, and turned to face him. Or rather, she turned toward the exit and was going to walk right past him as if he were invisible.

He planned to stop her—but then her eyes narrowed, she dropped the wood to the floor, and kicked it like a ball. He realized then that it was a skateboard. He was turning to see what she was doing when her sharp voice echoed in the quiet lobby.

"Take cover!"

She caught him off balance. Her surprisingly strong arms and compact body pushed him off his feet. At the same time, the all too familiar sound of gunfire erupted. He hit the ground and she rolled over him, landing in a crouch with both hands pressed firmly against the polished floor and one leg stretched out.

"Run when I tell you," she ordered, her violet eyes blazing with an unusually calm fire.

He conveyed his own experience and competence with a glance and noted that Tarek and the bodyguards had drawn their weapons and were firing. Tarek never missed.

"Qadir, this way," Tarek said in an urgent voice.

Qadir rose to his feet in one fluid motion. The woman started away from him, and he automatically captured her arm to keep her by his side. She frowned and tugged, trying to free herself.

"You got them. I've got to go," she said.

The high-pitched sound of sirens told him that someone had already reported the incident. Reporters would cover the building in minutes once they knew who the target was. The woman yanked her arm again, trying to break free with a new sense of urgency that made him frown.

"You'll come with me," he stated.

"Qadir, your hand. You're injured?" Tarek exclaimed.

She had opened her mouth to protest, but at Tarek's words, the woman's mouth snapped shut and she looked—irritated! Qadir followed the direction of his brother's gaze. Bright red blood could be seen between his fingers.

"The blood is not mine. Tarek, call my physician." he ordered.

"Your guy is going to need some help," she observed with approval. "The gunmen must not have hit an artery, otherwise he would've bled out by now."

Qadir listened in disbelief as this woman ignored the fact that she had been shot. Instead of being hysterical, she was acting as if nothing had happened. All around them, women had been screaming and many were now crying and hyperventilating from the terror of their close call. Hell, even some of the men were weeping like babes. The only thing he could rationalize was that she was in shock.

"This doctor is for you. Nizar will be seen by someone else," he growled.

He guided her with a hand at the small of her back and they entered the elevator. He looked down with amazed bewilderment at the top of her head. She could actually be his *Almukhtar*. She might have just saved his life. He couldn't even tell what color her hair was. It was completely covered by the knitted sock hat that she had pulled down over her ears.

He narrowed his eyes, wanting to pull it off and see her clearly. She absently held her arm, making herself even smaller than she already was. She barely came up to his chest.

"I need my board," she suddenly said.

He frowned, trying to comprehend. "Your board?" he repeated.

She nodded. "My skateboard. I shoved it at the two lunatics downstairs before they started shooting. I need it back," she said, worrying her bottom lip.

Astonishment filled him again. She had just witnessed a shooting, had been shot, and she was worried about a piece of battered wood on wheels. It was clear as she spoke that she was distressed by the idea of losing it.

He turned to his brother. "Will you see that her board is retrieved and returned to her?" he quietly requested in Arabic.

Tarek gave him a questioning look. He shrugged in response. Now was not the time or the place to explain that his mission to America had changed. He had come for revenge and had discovered his future queen. He smiled crookedly.

As Tarek radioed downstairs for one of the bodyguards to retrieve the board, Qadir looked at the woman and sensed her growing fatigue. He wanted to comfort her, but the elevator wasn't large enough to pick her up. He would carry her once they reached the upper board room of his kingdom's newly acquired business. The silence was suddenly broken when the woman spoke again.

"So, do people normally try to kill you on Friday nights, or is today a special day?" she casually inquired.

The three men with him all turned and looked at her as if she had lost her mind. A chuckle slipped from him, and he shook his head. Her comment fit perfectly with what he had noticed of her personality so far.

He slipped his hand against her side and gently braced her as the elevator stopped. The two bodyguards exited first, making sure the floor was secure. Tarek stepped out next before he looked at Qadir and nodded.

Qadir scooped the unsuspecting woman up in his arms, ignoring her startled squeak of protest. He scowled when he realized how dainty she was under the cover of her bulky clothing.

"What the hell are you doing?" she demanded, glaring up at him.

He chuckled. "I thought it was obvious—I'm carrying you," he said.

He addressed Tarek in Arabic, ensuring that the doctor would be brought to Carthmen's office.

"Dr. Fuah is already on his way up," Tarek replied and then teasingly added, "I don't think she is impressed with your chivalry."

Qadir glanced down at the woman in his arms before refocusing on where they were heading. If the look in her eyes could kill, he would be dead.

He wanted to kiss her pinched lips, soften them until they opened under his, but he was fairly certain that if he tried, she would bite him.

Qadir looked at Tarek and asked, "Can you review the papers while I stay with her?"

Tarek gave him a startled look before he nodded. "Of course."

The woman sighed and yawned. "Are we there yet?" she asked, mimicking a bored child.

He looked down at her with amusement. "Yes, little one," he softly goaded, "we're there."

When her eyes blazed up into his, it occurred to him that with this woman in his life, he might never be bored again.

Three

"I recommend rest. She should also be seen by her local physician. The wound should be kept dry for the next seven-to-ten days, or until the stitches are removed," Dr. Fuah said.

The woman looked at her arm, turning it back and forth with an appreciative gleam in her eyes as if she had just won a trophy for best injury of the day. Qadir didn't know whether to be exasperated by the confounding woman or amused. She refused to tell him her name.

"Call me Wheels," she had responded with a delicate shrug of her shoulders.

"Wheels? What kind of name is that?"

She had given him that pixie grin of hers, her eyes mischievous, and replied, "The best kind."

She had even refused to relent to Dr. Fuah's gentle inquisition. She had joked with the doctor as she removed the outer layers of her clothing so he could attend the wound. She removed each piece of clothing as if she were doing a stealthy striptease for Qadir, and her eyes dared him to leave. He *would* have left if she hadn't suggested he might want to stay in case she needed him to hold her hand. The sarcasm in her voice had been as thick as her challenge.

He gritted his teeth. The worst part was that she was completely aware of the effect she had on him. She wielded the unique magic of her eyes like a sword. Her magnetic weapon of choice trailed a path down his body with the same casualness as the movement of her fingers when she unfastened each button on her faded blue blouse.

He caught his breath when she dropped her left sleeve and revealed the wound on her upper arm to the doctor. She wasn't wearing a bra. Her lips were curled in a secret smile as she made eye contact with him and held the material so that it barely covered the creamy mound of her breast. All the while, her eyes danced with mirth—and defiance.

"You do sweet work, Doc. I don't think I'll have much of a scar to show off to the boys when it's healed," she commented, skillfully sliding her shirt back up and buttoning it, showing nothing she didn't want to.

A grumble of displeasure slipped from him before he could contain it, and he resisted the urge to kiss the amusement from her lips when she gave him a silent look of admonishment. Fortunately, Dr. Fuah missed their provocative exchange since his focus was on her wound, not the wicked thoughts dancing through her mind.

"I'm concerned—" Dr. Fuah began.

"I'm healthy as a horse, Doc. Don't you worry about me," she said, pulling on her coat.

"Dr. Fuah, I would like to speak with you for a moment—alone," Qadir stated.

"Yes… yes, sire," Dr. Fuah replied.

"I will return shortly," he informed her.

"I look forward to it," she purred, a wicked light gleaming in her eyes again.

SOMETHING ABOUT AIMEE

Qadir turned and exited the room, followed by Dr. Fuah. He had met some of the most beautiful, experienced women in the world, and made love to his share of them, but none had ever challenged him. None had ever flirted with him and dismissed him at the same time. It was as if the woman—Wheels—had been born without the self-preservation gene—as proven by her behavior earlier when she faced down the gunmen.

"What are you concerned about?" he demanded, turning to the elderly, plump doctor who had been his personal physician since he was a boy.

"I'm concerned about how thin she is, and I noticed older wounds on her body."

Qadir stilled and looked at the closed door behind Fuah. "What kind of old wounds?"

"A knife wound and another gunshot wound that have healed and left scars. She also has a large bruise on her shoulder that I would say is perhaps a week old. I'm concerned that she may be a victim of domestic violence."

Qadir's swiftly inhaled breath sounded loud in his ears.

"She appeared to want you there. Perhaps she will open up to you, sire," Fuah mused.

"I will take care of the matter," Qadir quietly declared. "What do you need for a more complete physical exam?"

Dr. Fuah's lips twitched in amusement. "Her approval—and perhaps some privacy."

Qadir bowed his head in acknowledgement and embarrassment. He should have known that nothing escaped the man's notice.

"Once she is on the plane, I will ensure you have everything you need —as long as I get a full report."

"*If* you get her on the plane, then I will be ready—with her permission, of course," Dr. Fuah responded with a chuckle. "Something tells me, sire, that she might not be easy to persuade."

"Since when has a woman ever turned me down?"

"Never, sire. If you are finished with my services, I would like to check on Nizar. I'm not sure I trust your finest guards with the American emergency medical system."

"Of course," he replied.

Qadir looked at the door again, replaying in his mind every moment he'd had with his mystery woman. He smiled in anticipation.

Turning the handle, he entered the office, stopped, and cursed. She was gone!

Aimee stepped out of the elevator. The lobby was full of men and women in blue, detectives, and emergency medical crew. Outside, a media frenzy was brewing. Aimee stood behind a large fake plant and warily watched the craziness. When she saw her skateboard on the reception counter, a bright yellow evidence tag attached to one wheel, a pleased grin curved her lips.

Crouching, she slipped around the tall plant, ducked behind the counter, and grabbed the board with her good arm. She snipped off the evidence tag with a pair of scissors and almost tossed it in the trash before she decided it would be a fun memento of a crazy day. She also pocketed the uneaten apple left from the receptionist's lunch. Slipping back behind the plant, she headed for the stairwell exit leading to the parking garage.

A blast of cold air hit her when she pushed open the door, and she shivered. She needed to run an errand before she headed home. Exiting the garage, she tossed the skateboard ahead of her and jumped on it.

Her mind wasn't on the bright lights or the crowds of pedestrians as she weaved in and out of them. It was on the tall, dark, and sexy man she had played Knight in Shining Armor with. She knew she was playing with fire, but she couldn't seem to help herself. It was the first time in her twenty-one years of life that she had actually found a guy worthy of her interest.

She grinned as she remembered her mom sweetly declaring that Aimee had been born with the soul of a Viking, the smarts of a Roman, and the strength of a Queen. Aimee snorted fondly. She wasn't *that* full of herself. She just knew who she was and what she wanted. Her life had always been unorthodox, and she wanted... someone who could match her, somehow, but surprise her too. Someone maybe like Qadir.

Aimee was happy being Wheels, the courier, delivery person, stocker, and a hundred other jobs that she had done. The only jobs she had avoided were being a waitress and a taxi driver. She didn't have the patience for the first one and she didn't have a driver's license. She had never needed one. Besides, skateboards were a lot cheaper to operate.

She was happy with her freedom, and she was willing to keep it going with jobs many would find unsavory. There were lines she wouldn't cross, but mostly, as long as it didn't get her killed, she would gladly take the variety of this life over the ball and chain trapping that very sexy man.

They were definitely *not* the same, and they wouldn't be in each other's orbit for very long. Still, they could have some adventures together, maybe.

She smiled.

Her tattered shoe touched the ground, propelling her forward. She wove around the trash in the alley like it was an obstacle course. When she came out the other end, she hung a left, and kicked her board up, catching it with her left hand. A sharp pain reminded her of the stitches in her arm.

It could have been a lot worse. Fortune had been on their side. He had been in the midst of turning toward the door, so he was off balance. If he hadn't been, there was no way she would have been able to knock him off his feet and out of the way of the bullet that hit her instead. She suspected that without her intervention he would have been shot in his upper back, hitting either a lung, his heart, or shattering his spine.

It had been a surprise when she hit him and discovered how firm he was under his designer clothing. She couldn't deny that she had judged him in the same way he had judged her. That realization, of course, made the encounter even more amusing.

What impressed her the most, though, was what happened after she rolled off him. He had been calm and focused, something that most of the professional guys she knew wouldn't have been.

The only ones she knew who could handle a crisis well were those forged by fire in the darkest regions of human society. Only the battle-hardened have experienced the adrenaline high and fought back— well, the battle-hardened and sociopaths.

Aimee was no sociopath. Yolanda used to tell her she was a piece of sunshine that got trapped on Earth. She spread her light to the darkest corners and brightened the world. Aimee shook her head at the memory. She would need to place another flower in the river tomorrow for Yolanda.

She entered her favorite market, cradling her board against her side so she could carry a shopping basket and still have a hand free.

"Aimee! You are late tonight," Mrs. Yang greeted with a smile.

"Yáng lǎobǎn wǎnshàng hǎo," *Good evening, Mrs. Yang,* Aimee responded.

"You had a good day?" Mrs. Yang asked in Mandarin.

"Yes, it was good. Peter bet I couldn't make a delivery in time," she replied with a tongue-in-cheek smile.

Mrs. Yang chuckled, and her eyes danced with delight. "How much did you win from him this time?"

"Twenty," Aimee replied, not going into the specifics of how the betting was done or split.

SOMETHING ABOUT AIMEE

Aimee walked along the narrow aisle of the Chinese market that Mr. and Mrs. Yang owned. She paused to pick up a package of dry noodle soup and a bottle of water before she rounded the end and squatted. She placed the aged basket on the floor and considered the selection of cat food.

She ignored the sound of the bell when the door opened. Placing a dozen different cans in the basket, she paused when she heard a deep, familiar voice. Pure hatred poured through her.

"Hello, Mrs. Yang," the honey-smooth voice greeted.

"Collection is not until tomorrow. I do not have payment ready yet," Mrs. Yang replied in a trembling voice.

"Payment is due at the end of the month."

"Yes, and tomorrow is the last day of the month," Mrs. Yang murmured.

"If I have to come back tomorrow, it will cost you another hundred for my time."

Mrs. Yang's soft cry of fear sent Aimee into motion. She gritted her teeth and walked up the aisle to the cash register. Her malevolent gaze locked on one of New York's lowest forms of life—a crooked cop.

Detective Anderson Coldhouse was a piece of shit. He had only been in this precinct for a few months, but he had been bad from the start. He had probably been doing horrible things somewhere else, got caught, and his superiors had transferred him here with a promotion instead of firing him—or arresting him.

Coldhouse turned when she plopped the basket on the counter, his eyes widening with disbelief as she literally pushed him aside.

"Mrs. Yang, do you have any more of the Seafood-flavored cat food?" Aimee inquired.

"I believe we have more in the back," Mrs. Yang said.

"Can you look? I grabbed the last two cans and need two more," Aimee asked with a smile.

"Yes, yes, please, give me a moment," Mrs. Yang said, hurrying to the back of the store.

Aimee turned and looked Coldhouse in the eye. "Nice night. I heard that someone was filing a complaint about some crooked cops shaking down immigrant store owners. You wouldn't know anything about that, would you?"

Coldhouse looked at her with narrowed eyes. She lifted her chin.

"I don't think that would be a good idea," he coolly responded.

"Yeah, well, I don't think it's a good idea for anyone to abuse their position of power. Who knows what could happen to them, right?" she quipped.

Mrs. Yang returned with the two cans of cat food Aimee had requested and a white envelope. As she stepped back behind the counter, Mrs. Yang's anxious eyes fluttered back and forth between Aimee and Coldhouse. She silently handed the envelope to Coldhouse before she began ringing up Aimee's purchases.

Coldhouse stuffed the envelope into his pocket and leaned closer to Aimee. "Watch your back, street rat. *I've* heard that it's open season on rodents who can't keep their mouths shut."

Aimee's eyes remained locked on Coldhouse as he exited the store and climbed into a waiting car.

The car pulled away, she took a deep breath, and her rage banked enough for her to realize that she was standing there with her fingers curled into a fist.

If only she could—

She shook her head. *What? End up in the river like Yolanda?*

"Aimee, you must be careful," Mrs. Yang said in a soft voice.

Aimee turned and smiled at Mrs. Yang. "Always," she promised, handing the gentle storekeeper the money she owed. "Have a good night, Mrs. Yang. Tell your hubby I said hello."

"I will," Mrs. Yang promised.

Aimee adjusted her load, placing the bag of groceries into her courier bag, and pulled the door open. She stepped out into the cold night air and breathed deeply. After lowering her skateboard to the ground, she took off, disappearing into the maze of streets and alleys.

Ten minutes later, she slipped between the locked gates of an abandoned riverfront warehouse with a large 'For Sale' sign on them. She crossed the dark parking area, her eyes skillfully scanning the darkness for any threats. She carefully made her way around the building, checking each door and possible entrance. Rounding the building to the waterfront side, she climbed up a stack of pallets to a grime-coated window.

She ran her fingers along the edge to the piece of paper she had stuck in it. The paper was still there—her home was safe. She pulled the paper free, climbed through the window, and latched it behind her. She jumped down off the box under the window, wincing when she jarred her arm.

Almost immediately, she heard many tiny padded feet and the excited meows of her furry roommates. She chuckled when seven felines swarmed around her, weaving between her legs. The momma cat and her six kittens gave Aimee all the companionship she needed.

She walked across the warehouse to a set of stairs leading up to what used to be the main office area. She crouched, opened her courier bag, and exchanged the empty cans of cat food with fresh ones. The kittens quickly abandoned her for their evening meal.

She deposited the old cans in a trash can next to the stairs and looked at the kittens. They were growing so fast! She had taken up residence here only three months ago, and they were already half the size of their mother.

She climbed the stairwell to the upper office and checked to make sure the paper was at the top of the door before she opened it. Her security system might be rudimentary, but it was functional—and it had saved her life more than once.

She closed the door behind her. The momma cat and kittens would find a way in if they wanted to snuggle during the night. They always did. She draped her bag on an old office chair and walked to her makeshift bed. She toed off her battered shoes.

"Nothing lasts forever," she said with a sigh before she picked up the runners and tossed them with the skill of a professional basketball player into the trash can.

She lit the small single burner camp stove, filled the pot with water from the bottle she had bought, and placed the apple and dried noodle soup on the desk.

While the water heated, she walked over to a leaning metal bookcase and pulled a shoebox down from the top. Opening the box, she looked inside and smiled at the new bright red high-top sneakers she had purchased last week. They would last her until she wore them out.

She placed them next to the bed. The water was already boiling. She pulled back the paper lid on the soup, and poured the hot water into it, then she carried the soup, a plastic spork, and her apple back to her bed.

The quilted bedspread was old, but clean. It was too cold to get undressed. She would get into work early and shower there. The shower was definitely a necessity for a courier service. Too many of them got drenched, muddy, or bloodied after a harried day. It even had hot water.

She slipped between the covers, piled the blankets on top, and wrapped her hands around the hot container to warm them. It was going to be a brutal winter if the early drop in temperatures was anything to go by. If she were smart, she would seriously consider becoming a snowbird.

She pulled out the travel magazine she had found two days earlier in a trash can and thumbed through it. Sun-filled beaches under blue skies greeted her. The day's tension slowly seeped away as she read the articles, drinking up the exotic places as the soup warmed her empty stomach.

The first soft meow made her smile. By the time her dinner was finished, the kittens had climbed up and burrowed under the covers with her. Soon, the momma cat, a little more hesitant than her offspring, joined them.

Aimee leaned back, trying to finish the article, but she was too tired and comfy to stay awake. She reached over, turned off the small, battery-powered light on her makeshift nightstand, and placed the magazine next to it. She snuggled down, pulling her knit cap over her ears to keep them warm, and rolled onto her side, folding her hands under her cheek.

Breathing deeply, she closed her eyes. A slight smile curved her lips when the image of Qadir formed her in mind. She wondered if he was thinking of her. Images of them on one of the sun-kissed beaches, the warm waters lapping at their feet as they made love, filled her mind.

This will be a good dream, she decided, letting the beauty of the moment sweep her away from her refrigerator cold home and into his warm, strong embrace.

Four

Aimee was almost within sight of Becker's Courier Services when she saw Peter biking quickly toward her from up ahead, hollering, "Hey, Wheels!"

She wondered with amusement what the drama was this time. He slid sideways to a stop on the bicycle.

"You've got a ghost," he announced. His heavy breathing formed a thick fog in the cold air.

Aimee slid her foot lightly along the sidewalk to slow her skateboard. "Who is it?" she asked.

Peter shrugged. "Don't know. Carl says it's the Feds. Polly thinks it's the Mafia. Since you've probably pissed off both, I'm not betting on either one."

Aimee resisted rolling her eyes at him. "Fat lot of good you are. Can you at least describe them? That might help me narrow down if I'm about to do time in the slammer or wear new concrete boots for the winter," she dryly stated.

"I dunno. Tall, dark, foreign-looking, bathing in money. Guess that rules out the Feds. I'll go with the Mafia," Peter said with a shrug.

Aimee's heart skipped. "Not Mafia. Middle East somewhere," she guessed.

Peter raised a skeptical eyebrow. "You trying to rule out *any* safe place to hide?" he quipped.

She did roll her eyes at that comment. "You remember the shooting down at the Harris building last week?"

He nodded. "Yeah. You saw it?"

She grinned. "I not only saw it, I might have tackled some rich dude and saved his life."

"You're shitting me, right? I heard that two guys came in and were iced by this Sheikh's bodyguards. I never heard anything about a lowly courier from Becker's being involved," Peter exclaimed.

"Not only involved, I've got the stitches from being shot to prove it," she boasted with a twinkle in her eye.

"Damn it."

"You keep betting against me, you'll never be able to get out of here," she teased.

Peter gave her a crooked grin. "I'm not paying until I see the evidence. Piggy may still have you beat. He had to have three pins in his ankle."

Aimee shook her head. "Piggy broke his ankle when he stepped off a curb while eating a hot dog. Self-damage through inattentiveness does not count."

"So, do you think he's here to give you a big thank you reward for saving his life?" Peter curiously asked.

Aimee shrugged. "I hope not. As much as I could use it, I've got a policy about not taking rewards for doing the right thing."

"You've got a really messed up code of honor, girl. Just promise me if he offers you a million dollars, you'll give it to me. I don't think so highly of myself that I would turn it down," Peter said.

"I'll consider it," she dryly replied before motioning for him to start pedaling. "How about a lift back?"

Peter snorted, but kicked off. Aimee grabbed the back of his seat and let him pull her along the uneven sidewalk.

She didn't bother hiding the pleased smile when she saw the trio of vehicles parked in front of Stanley's place. The long limousine's windows were dark in the back so she couldn't see who was inside, but she knew who it would be.

She released the back of Peter's bike and glided over the cement, her attention moving from the limo to the door when a familiar figure appeared. Her smile grew as she came to a stop a couple of feet in front of him.

"It's nice to see you're still in one piece without me there to save you," she teased.

Heat rushed through Qadir the moment he saw Aimee gliding on her skateboard behind the tall, lanky man who had rushed out of Becker's Courier Services minutes before. He devoured her with his gaze, assessing that she was alright. The frustrations of the past week melted away under the intensity of her brilliant, infectious smile.

His discussion with Stanley Becker had been brief. The old man was hard as nails and more protective than a Pitbull. The man wouldn't even tell him her full name. He was beginning to wonder if anyone knew it. The investigator his brother hired had discovered nothing— no birth certificate, no Social Security card, no driver's license, not even a library card. It was as if the woman didn't exist—yet here she was, at last.

"You have not been at work," he said.

Mischief gleamed in her eyes and he could have sworn she was *'amirat khurafia,* a fairy princess, casting her spell on him. He was a willing conquest for his mysterious sprite. Tarek's words of caution hadn't dampened his enthusiasm the slightest bit.

"I've been at work, just not delivering the messages you've been sending," she stated, kicking her skateboard and catching it in midair.

With exasperation, he grasped her slender waist, which was once again camouflaged by the worn, baggy coat she wore, and looked into her eyes. She warmed his blood, and he was certain she felt the same shock of awareness that he did.

"Why?" he asked in a low voice.

The expression in her eyes softened. "Because you weren't sending the right one."

Qadir briefly closed his eyes and muttered a curse in Arabic, thankful that she wouldn't understand what he was saying.

"There is a dinner tonight. I would like you to attend it with me," he said.

Her peal of warm laughter made her cheeks flush a rosy shade.

He tilted his head in defiant bemusement. If he weren't a supremely confident man, a response like hers might make him worry. At least, that was what he told himself as he worried.

When her laughter died, her own bemusement showed in the smile that curved her lips.

"I might be a little underdressed for any party you invite me to," she said softly with a shake of her head.

"I do not even know what color your hair is," he suddenly said, fingering her knitted cap.

She tugged the cap further down on her head. The challenging look was back in her eyes, but then she studied him curiously. She slid her hand over his.

"If you want to see my hair, you'll have to tell me when and where the party is. I'll be there," she promised.

He smiled with satisfaction, though his confusion at her assumptions showed in his eyes. "I will send a car for you, of course. As far as clothing is concerned, pick out anything you wish at LaClaire's and have them place it on my account."

She raised an eyebrow. "And how does that work? Can any old street bum walk into LaClaire's and order up an outfit?"

"I will inform Chantel you will be coming. Call me if you need anything," he said, pulling a black business card from his pocket. "It has my direct line."

Aimee slowly took the card from him. With wary confusion, she glanced at his face and then examined the card before sliding it into her pocket.

"I have to go now," Qadir said with regret, "but I will see you this evening. Call the number on the front of the card and give my assistant your address. Unfortunately, I will be in meetings and will not be there myself to pick you up, but I will wait with bated breath for you at the Mayor's Annual Ball."

"A Ball…" she softly exclaimed. After a moment, she gave the ground a small, lopsided smile as she refused to look at him.

He touched her chin, tilting her head up. "You will be the most beautiful woman there no matter what you wear, *habibi*," he murmured.

Her smile was bright and pleased, if still a little disbelieving. She shook her head playfully as Qadir released her and stepped back.

"Trying to be both my fairy godmother and my Prince Charming? What an overachiever," she teased.

He laughed and resisted the urge to tell her exactly what he wanted to be for her—and do *to* her. He bowed his head respectfully and returned to his car.

The bodyguard closed the door. Qadir's gaze remained locked on Wheels. He hadn't dared kiss her goodbye. He knew if he did, he would not return to his meetings.

If tonight went as he planned, his beautiful *'amirat khurafia* would not be returning to this dismal job, which didn't pay her enough to wear decent attire.

Pulling his phone out, he dialed LaClaire's. His *'amirat khurafia* needed more than just one dress. He would clothe her in the finest New York had to offer.

Then I will peel each piece off of her, he thought.

"Spill it, who was the hotty?" Polly demanded the moment Aimee entered the workroom.

Aimee laughed. Everyone had their eyes glued to her like she had just sprouted wings—or horns. She clutched the little black card in her pocket as if it was a magic ticket. The only problem was… she wanted to do this on her terms, not his.

"I need your help," she said.

"Name it," Carl said, tilting his head back and grinning.

"Did he give you a million dollars? I can help you spend it," Peter said.

Aimee laughed. Polly tried to hit Peter, but he ducked and danced over to Aimee, wrapping his arm around her shoulders. She leaned against him.

"What do you need, Wheels?" Stanley asked.

She gazed at them with wide eyes. "Everything. I've been invited to a ball tonight."

The crowd around her burst into conversation. Polly's squeal of delight mixed with Carl and Peter's groans of dismay. Aimee giggled when the inevitable joke was made about turning her skateboard into a carriage and the three guys into footmen. Polly gushed about finding the perfect dress for the occasion. Even Stanley added his two cents. In the end, Aimee had all the help she needed to make this ball special.

Polly's Aunt Eddy welcomed Aimee into her vintage boutique, and she borrowed a full length silk, sequin and bead embellished ballgown from the turn of the 20th century that was the same deep violet color of her eyes.

The dress had three-quarter sleeves that hid most of her scars and the wound from last week. Aimee had removed the stitches the night before. The bodice of the dress was tight against her small breasts. Delicate beads and tiny pearls decorated the bodice while an overlay of sequins molded the dress to her slender waist and flowed over her hips. The dress flared out behind her.

Eddy produced a pair of cream-colored demi boots with pearl buttons and low, wide heels.

"Can't have you slipping, sliding, or tripping on some slick polished floor. The women of old knew how to protect their ankles," Eddy said with a prim nod of her head. "Now take off the dress and let Polly take care of your hair."

Polly worked as a beautician when she wasn't working at Becker's. Polly and Eddy breathed an exclamation of awe as Polly unwound Aimee's very long, black curly hair.

Yolanda used to say that she had been gifted with the tresses of a fairy-tale princess and begged her to never cut it. Yolanda had spent hours brushing her hair and braiding it. Aimee did the same. As a result, her hair flowed like a shimmering curtain down past her derriere.

"Girl, I can't believe you keep this hidden under that disgusting cap!"

Aimee laughed. "I don't think me flying down 5th Avenue looking like a wild woman would be conducive to a long and healthy life. One snag in a taxi and I'd be bald."

"You'd make a gorgeous model," Polly countered.

Aimee laughed. "I can hear it now 'Ladies and Gentlemen, for the tiny gnomes of the fashion world, here is Wheels, the death-defying, wild woman of New York and her trusty skateboard,'" Aimee said, imitating a deep-voiced announcer.

Eddy and Polly laughed and teased her about her wild-woman persona. It was a fun four hours to get ready, and now Aimee felt like a princess as she settled into the horse-drawn carriage Stanley had arranged for her. She curled her fingers in the vintage muff and tried to refrain from thinking about the demise of the poor animal who had been sacrificed to make it.

Polly had insisted on her leaving her hair down, and it certainly helped keep away the chill from the open air. Her cloak helped more. Aimee's face was almost completely concealed by the hood of the cloak and the lavish fur-trimming.

The ball was at the Waldorf Astoria. She breathed a sigh when the carriage driver smoothly maneuvered the silver and white carriage between two limousines. She had arrived.

"I hope you have a wonderful evening, Wheels," Stanley's brother said as he drew his horse to a standstill in front of the golden doors.

"Thank you, Franklin—for everything," she breathlessly replied as she rose to her feet.

A doorman rushed forward and opened the carriage door for her. Aimee extended her hand, the doorman firmly grasped it, and she lifted her long skirt as she stepped down, out of the carriage.

Several men outside the venue stopped to gawk at her. Their glances started out as casual curiosity, but quickly became intense stares that spared no regard for their own dates. Paparazzi turned like a swarm of locusts, snapping pictures with blinding lights.

Aimee sparkled in the brightly lit entrance, her cream-colored cloak richly embellished with white pearls and tiny amethyst gems. Murmurs of speculation as to who she was rippled through the crowds. Aimee didn't bother hiding the grin that she figured no one could see under her hood. She almost wished she could magically turn back into her usual self just to see their faces.

Still, for one night, she would be Qadir's Cinderella. A doorman and the mayor of the city opened the doors for her. She swept through with a smile and a husky thank you. Amusement touched her smile when she noticed a few men trying to suck in their guts as she entered the ballroom.

Then she saw him, and Aimee's breath caught in her chest for a moment before it broke free. Qadir wasn't quite the tallest man in the room, but he was the handsomest. As he impatiently scanned the room, she studied him. His blue-black hair was pulled back and tied at his nape. The coal black tailcoat was tailored to perfection for his broad shoulders and lithe body.

"Your cloak, ma'am," a clerk requested.

Aimee nodded and passed the clerk her hand muff, not taking her eyes off of Qadir. He turned, his eyes locking on her as she pulled back her hood.

The look he gave her was scorching. In his expression, the fire of desire battled with a steadying relief. She felt the same as she unhooked the fastenings on the cloak, letting it slide off her shoulders.

The clerk caught her cloak and handed her a ticket. She slid it into the cream-colored beaded pocketbook Eddy had given her.

"Thank you," she murmured to the clerk, already stepping forward.

The crowd parted as if by magic, their eyes on the dazzling young woman with flowing black hair that seemed to cup her derriere. She was different, ethereal in a dress that was as timelessly beautiful as she was.

Aimee's smile grew brighter, outshining the largest diamond in the room, as Qadir strode with long, determined strides toward her. Her lips parted at the promise held within the depths of his dark chocolate eyes. Before she could greet him, he wrapped his arms around her, and kissed her with a passion that nearly set the room ablaze.

Aimee could feel her knees tremble. She would have made a spectacular puddle of purple silk and sequins if not for Qadir's strong arms holding her up. She wound her arms around his neck and returned his kiss as if she would die without it.

A soft sigh slipped from her when he slowly ended the kiss. She looked up at him, her lips swollen and moist, and gave him a crooked, mischievous smile.

"I guess you like my hair," she murmured.

He twirled a small tendril of her thick tresses around his finger and lifted it to his cheek, looking at her as he nuzzled against the softness of it.

"I want to wrap myself in it and tie you to me, *'amirati alkhayalia*," he replied in a voice filled with barely restrained need.

A shudder of desire went through her, threatening to send her into an orgasm right there and then if she didn't defuse the situation.

"If you do, we'll both be posting bail and explaining to the judge in the morning why we burned New York down—or at least the Waldorf," she joked, slowly pushing against his shoulder.

He grunted in response, straightened, and reluctantly released her. The surrounding crowds breathed a sigh and a low murmur filled the air again. He touched her back and guided her across the room to a surprisingly private area.

"I was worried that you would not come," he admitted.

"What… and miss all of this… and that hot kiss?"

Five

A Few Minutes Earlier

Qadir's steely glance swept over the gathering crowd. He murmured appropriate responses when necessary to those seeking an audience with him, but behind his polite mask, disbelief raged with disappointment. His *'amirat khurafia* had promised she would be here. His cell phone vibrated. He retrieved it from his pocket and read the message.

> Nothing. She never showed up at LaClaire's. Karam never received a call. It would appear your mystery lady has disappeared again.

Tarek didn't add what he had been saying over and over to Qadir—that maybe it would be for the best to let this one slip through his fingers. He knew that Tarek was worried about the earlier attack and the role his mysterious woman had played in it. The two dead attackers had been street thugs. To date, Tarek couldn't find a link to any of Qadir's known enemies.

What was even more perplexing was how the woman knew what was going to happen so quickly. Was she part of the plan? She had disappeared before Tarek or the police could interrogate her. That, coupled with the fact she had no paper trail in a time when everyone did, cast even further doubt on her innocence.

He shoved his cellphone back into his pocket just as a feeling of awareness hit him. Turning, he scanned the room, searching for the source. He was on his second sweep when his eyes locked on a goddess walking into the room in a cream-colored cloak. Her face was shielded by the fur-trimmed hood, but he would know her anywhere.

She was looking at him as she handed her fur muff to the clerk standing near the door. He didn't realize he was holding his breath until she lifted her slender hands and pushed the hood back to reveal her face. The hum of voices faded into the background as she reached up and unfastened the catch on her cloak. It fell from her shoulders.

He was sure that every man in the room had been waiting for the same thing, to see what she was wearing—or not wearing—under the cover of her cloak. His body hardened at the thought, and he came close to charging across the room, sweeping her into his arms, and carrying her off.

The vintage gown she was wearing was breathtaking in the way it accentuated her slender figure, molding to her curves, capturing the light as she stood still. For a moment, he wondered if she was real.

Her glorious dark hair cascaded in stunning silky waves down her back. He had fantasized about what her hair might look like, but nothing could have prepared him for the reality.

He started forward at the same time she did. His passion grew exponentially along with his need to announce to every man here that she belonged to him. The smile on her face lit up the room, and he feared some poor, misguided soul would make the fatal error of getting between him and the vision walking toward him.

When her lips parted to speak, he lost the last thread of his control and captured them in a kiss that could rival the greatest kisses ever filmed.

She opened for him like a flower, beguiling him with her heat, her softness, her taste. Her soft moan sent triumph galloping through him, and when she wound her arms around his neck, he barely resisted urging her to wrap her legs around him too.

It took him several seconds to regain enough awareness of his surroundings to realize the scene they were creating. He reluctantly ended their kiss, only managing it because he promised himself this kiss was only the first of many more to come.

"I guess you like my hair," she murmured.

Their ensuing banter did nothing to calm his raging libido. She wanted him as much as he wanted her. She admitted it. He breathed deeply and straightened.

He could be a civilized date for this extraordinary woman, he told himself. She deserved that much. He released her and stepped back.

When he led her into the crowd, though, he couldn't help wondering how quickly he could get them out of here.

"Where did you get that dress?" he asked, his eyes on the soft mounds of her breasts.

She followed his gaze before tilting her head to look up at him with that smile of hers that drove him crazy. Qadir's fingers tightened on her elbow when she made each of her breasts move. A choked laugh slipped from him, and he shook his head.

"It's pretty amazing, isn't it? I don't always wear a bra, and in this thing, I definitely didn't need one."

"Do you enjoy torturing me?" he growled, looking around to see if anyone had overheard her.

Her delighted laughter was like a siren's song. Every damn man within a twenty-foot radius who hadn't already been mesmerized by the gorgeous nymph *must* be by now. He sent a glare around the room, ready to fight off anyone who got too close to her, but the party continued as usual, if slightly more hushed and with more glances sent their way. Odd. He couldn't be the only one who felt like a madman in her presence.

"Did you know the mayor actually opened the door for me?"

He looked across the room to where the mayor was standing. The man's eyes were glued on Qadir's... on... 'Wheels'. With frustration, Qadir looked at his stubborn, mystery woman who was now holding a glass of champagne.

"What is your name, *'amirati alkhayalia?*" he asked.

She peered up at him through her lashes. "Is it that important? Everyone calls me Wheels," she said.

He shook his head. "I do not want to call you Wheels when I am making love to you." He caressed her cheek with the back of his fingers.

Her pupils dilated, and she ran the tip of her tongue over her lips.

"I like it when you call me *'amirati alkhayalia,*" she murmured.

"*Please, 'amirati alkhayalia.*"

She studied his face before she motioned with her finger for him to come closer. He leaned forward. She slid her hand along his cheek and turned her head until her lips almost touched his ear.

"When you make love to me, you can call me Aimee," she whispered.

She flicked the lobe of his ear with the tip of her tongue. He drew in a sharp breath, and she stepped back, taking a sip of her champagne.

Her name flowed through his mind. He rolled it over his tongue. His eyes were drawn to her flushed cheeks. It took him a moment to realize that she wasn't wearing any makeup. The realization tugged at his heart. She was a woman who screamed 'take me as I am or not at all'.

"Let's get out of here," he said.

Her eyes widened, and she looked around. "But… the party hasn't even started yet, has it?"

He took the glass from her hand and brought his lips close to hers, his eyes blazing with need.

"Tell me you don't want this," he challenged softly. "Tell me you'd rather stay here all night where I can only tease us both, instead of stroking every tantalizing inch of you beneath your dress."

Aimee gasped. She decisively took her glass from Qadir and placed it on the tray of a passing server. Smiling with anticipation, Qadir cupped her hand in his, and turned her toward the main entrance.

He pulled his cell phone out and pressed a button. "Pull the car around now," he ordered.

He signaled the clerk to bring their coats, and he valiantly ignored the overeager clerk's lingering looks at Aimee. Qadir politely accepted their property from the kid who didn't even look old enough to shave.

"My men will shield you as much as possible as we leave. Keep moving forward and get in the limousine," he instructed.

She nodded, pulling the hood of her cloak up and taking her fur hand muff. "You know, we could avoid all of that if we just go down two floors, take the staff entrance to the side alley, and have your guy pick us up on the next block over," she suggested.

He stopped, looked at her, and shook his head. "Another question. You'll have to explain how you know that," he said. He redirected his driver to follow her instructions.

Gafar, one of his bodyguards, emerged from the crowd. Three more appeared once they left the ballroom. He kept his hand pressed against the small of Aimee's back. Her shorter legs kept up with him and his men.

When she lifted the skirt of her dress, he caught sight of the delicate, beaded ankle boots she was wearing. His lust surged again. There was not one damn thing about this woman that didn't drive him crazy.

Staff moved out of the way as they bustled through the corridors. Aimee directed them, pointing to a door when he thought they had reached a dead end. They emerged from the lower level. A short walk had them entering the street on the opposite side of the building.

Omar, one of the four bodyguards with him, rushed forward and opened the door of the limo. Aimee disappeared inside. Qadir followed, falling into her arms when she twisted on the seat and opened them.

He gathered her close. Her soft laughter made him feel warm and light-hearted. These were emotions he usually only experienced when he was riding along the coast or out in the desert. Once again, he was drowning in her unusual eyes.

"I want you," he stated.

"I know."

She pulled his head down and captured his lips. While she tangled her fingers in his hair, pulling it free of its binding, he groaned, sliding his hand down her side, searching for the hem of her dress. When the length of silk seemed to go on forever, he rumbled with frustration, but the obstacle did clear his head for a moment. He ended their kiss, pulling her into a sitting position.

"What's wrong?" she asked, sitting up and looking around.

"Several things," he chuckled, kissing her again. "The first time we are together, I don't want it to be in the backseat of a limousine like a couple of teenagers. I want to savor you. Second, once I finally get you out of that dress, I don't think it will be as easy to get it back on. If my bodyguard opens the door and you're not fully clothed, I'm afraid there might be violence," he ruefully added.

She wiggled her nose playfully. "I doubt many teenagers have a limo to make-out in." She laughed, glancing around the interior. "You know, this seat alone is bigger than the bed I sleep on. Of course, it is only me most of the time. You definitely wouldn't fit."

The intense jealousy that swept through him at the thought of Aimee with another man was familiar by now, though tonight was the first time he'd ever felt it. It had never bothered him with his previous lovers. In fact, he enjoyed the talents of an experienced lover. He would just have to make sure that he wiped the memory of her previous lovers from her mind. Lifting her hand to his mouth, he kissed her palm.

"Then it is a good thing my bed will be large enough for the both of us," he said.

"A very good thing," she agreed with a smile.

Six

Qadir ordered his bodyguards to give them privacy as he and Aimee entered the elevator. The moment the doors closed and they were alone, she turned into his arms with a wicked smile on her lips. By the time they reached his penthouse apartment, his outer coat and jacket were open, his tie undone, his shirt was pulled free and unbuttoned, and his pants half undone.

Aimee's hands were everywhere and so were his. The pearl buttons running down the back of her gown were undone, and he had one hand cupping her firm breast. He pinched her nipple and she went wild in his arms.

The doors opened into the foyer, and he pushed her cloak off her shoulders, catching it with one hand and draping it over a decorative entrance table. He slid the gown from her shoulders, not breaking their passionate kiss. The material pooled at her feet, leaving her bare except for her lacy panties and the pearl-studded ankle boots.

His breath left him for a moment.

"My beautiful angel," he murmured.

"You seriously have too many clothes on," she moaned.

He peeled off his outer coat and tossed it on the table. His shirt joined her dress on the floor. Toeing off his dress shoes, he removed the rest of his clothing until he was standing proudly in front of her. She wrapped her hand around his throbbing cock.

"Sweet desert rose, but you do enjoy torturing me," he groaned.

"Are you kidding? I haven't even started yet," she teased, raising her booted foot with a pointed look.

"I never wear shoes to bed," she said. She stroked his hard length before releasing him.

He inhaled through gritted teeth and obediently removed one of her boots, then the other. She rewarded him by bringing her small breasts closer to his lips. They were like delicate plums to be suckled, but he only breathed on them as he ran his hands up her thighs to the lacy edge of her panties.

"Now I'm wearing too much," she panted.

Qadir had never been seduced so skillfully and passionately before. He threaded his fingers beneath the thin straps of her underwear and pulled the lace down her legs until she stepped out of them. He tossed them aside, then retraced the path back to her hips and pulled her forward until he could bury his mouth against the soft curls protecting her lush mound.

"Holy… shit!" she exclaimed, pressing against him and holding on to his head.

He smiled. Aimee was a woman who knew what she wanted and took it without remorse. He loved it. The scent of her desire nearly made him forget his vow to take his pleasure slowly with her. He wanted nothing more than to bury himself to the hilt inside her and relieve this painful throb of need.

He parted her delicate folds, exposing the sensitive nub of her womanhood, and slid his fingers into her hot channel as he captured the nub with his lips. She rocked her hips in time with his tender strokes. Her loud, passionate moans caused the tip of his cock to moisten with desire.

She trembled and tightly clenched her fingers in his hair. He sensed she was about to come and wanted to revel in her sweet release as it washed over his tongue. Her loud cry filled him with triumph. He sucked on the nub, holding her by the buttocks when she struggled to break away from him.

"I can't... I can't... Oh... shit, I can." Her panting breaths filled his ears with the music of her orgasm.

Knowing he was close to coming, he cursed when he couldn't find his wallet and a condom. Rising to his feet, he decided the risk was worth it. He lifted her up and pressed her back against the wall, pushed his cock through her soft curls, and broke through the thin barrier of her virginity in a single thrust.

She gave a startled yelp of pain. Her wide, dazed eyes held a look of shock that must have matched his own. Her parted lips were swollen from his kisses. He moaned and captured her lips, fighting to stay still while her body adjusted to him.

A shudder ran through him when her feminine depths pulsed around him. She moved her hips, as if testing to see if there would be more pain. She relaxed her fingers, her nails no longer biting into the flesh of his shoulders, and she began to rock. He broke their kiss and buried his head against her shoulder.

"Aimee," he gritted.

"Oh, that's it. I love the feel of you inside me," she groaned, wrapping her arms around his head and holding him as she began to move faster.

Qadir braced his legs to keep from melting into the ground, and he gripped Aimee's thighs tighter. He knew she would carry the imprint of his fingers on her flesh tomorrow, but he couldn't help it. The feel of her silky channel stroking his hard cock was driving him out of his mind.

He was breathing heavily and began rocking with her. Ricocheting through him was the knowledge that this passionate woman in his arms was his—all his. She had never given this passion to anyone else. He pushed in as deeply as he could go and came with an intensity that left him reeling. He shuddered and gasped.

A moment passed with only their breathing breaking the silence, and it was wonderful.

"Aimee," he tenderly murmured. "We need to talk about what just happened."

"We can talk later. I want to do this again," she replied with a happy sigh.

Aimee carefully slipped from Qadir's embrace, tucking her warm pillow under his arm. She smiled tenderly and blew him a kiss. She was sure that if she kissed his skin and woke him up, she would never make it to work.

She rifled through his walk-in closet, finding a pair of workout pants with an elastic waist and tie string, a long-sleeve shirt, a black cashmere sweater, and a pair of thick socks. She dressed in the closet, chuckling as the oversized clothes made her normal ones appear form-fitting.

After finger-combing her tangled hair, she braided and wound it up, tucking the ends under the braid to hold it until she could retrieve the hairpins in her pocketbook. Peering into the bedroom, she saw Qadir was still sleeping deeply.

Blowing him another kiss, she tiptoed out of the bedroom. First she went for her hairpins, but in minutes, she had folded and stacked Qadir's discarded clothing on the foyer table and written a brief note to him, leaving it on top of the pile.

Using her cloak as a makeshift bag that enclosed her dress and pocketbook, she gathered her belongings into her arms, slipped her feet into her boots, and was about to step into the private elevator when she had a thought that made her pause. Slipping out of the building would be a little trickier than getting in had been. She knew that there would be bodyguards everywhere. The last thing she wanted to do was have them disturb Qadir.

Biting her lip, she figured there must be an emergency exit or a servants' elevator. A sudden memory made her smile with excitement. Her friend, Lucy, had worked as a housekeeper for a ritzy client in a private penthouse apartment. The cook had haughtily informed Lucy that she should never use the private elevator. Instead, Lucy was shown how to enter the apartment via a set of stairs that connected the floor below the penthouse to the kitchen.

Aimee located the kitchen and scanned it, eventually locating the small, red exit sign over a door that looked like it went into a pantry. Opening the door, she saw a narrow entranceway with a keypad. It would be alarm activated.

She grinned when she saw that whoever used it last had messy fingers. A thick paste of flour coated the keys that had been pressed first and more lightly dusted the keys pressed last. She pressed the sequence, hoping it was the right combination. The light turned green and the familiar click of an electronic lock opening made her grin.

"Thank you, messy fingers!" she breathed.

She pulled the door open, stepped out into the stairwell, and closed the door behind her, making sure it was locked before she headed down the stairs. One floor down, she came to another keypad. Punching in the same code, she grinned when the light turned green. She stepped into the hallway across from a service elevator.

Minutes later, she exited the building through the employee entrance and was embraced by the cold. Early morning delivery trucks were beginning their runs. Aimee clutched her bundle of belongings, lightly ran after one of the trucks that was pulling away from the kitchen area, and jumped onto the back, grasping the handle for support. Her ride wasn't much different from those of the firefighters or garage guys.

The cold chased away the fog in her brain and she breathed in the mixture of early morning air and city stench. This was her world, and she loved it! There was only one thing she loved more—Qadir!

Three different produce trucks and forty minutes later, Aimee punched in the code to Becker's Courier Service. She gathered a change of clothes from her locker, showered, dressed, and tried to get out as many wrinkles as possible from the clothes Polly had lent her before hanging them up.

She retrieved her skateboard, courier bag, and the envelope of money containing her bonus and her share of the winnings from the bet. She tucked the envelope into the front pocket of her jeans as she exited through the back door of the building. There were a few things she needed to do before the rest of the crew arrived and another busy work day began.

Seven

Qadir woke with a start when his hand touched the cool fabric of his bed linens. He sat up and looked around, searching for Aimee in the dim interior of his bedroom. Throwing the covers back, he rolled out of bed. His long strides took him into the bathroom. It was empty.

"Aimee!" he called.

Silence greeted him. His gaze moved back to the bed. He had been holding her pillow. Retracing his steps, he picked up the pillow and buried his face in it, desperately needing to know that last night had not been a dream. The faint fragrance of her shampoo still clung to the pillow.

A stain on the otherwise pristine sheets caught his attention. He lowered the pillow and pulled back the covers. The evidence of Aimee's innocence and their night together hit him like a fist in the gut.

He had not been dreaming. His passionate wildcat had been a virgin. He felt something raw and primitive surge through him. He knew it was ridiculous in this day and age to feel such a powerful—and some would argue inappropriate—sense of possessiveness, but he didn't care.

Aimee was his in every way. The powerful, instant attraction to her had shaken him, as did his recognition of her as his *Chosen*—the one meant to complete him—but all his inner turmoil and resistance to the idea had been a mere footnote as she led him on a merry chase, and he simply could not stop himself from going after her. He needed her. It was crazy.

There were those, even among his people, who would argue that what he was feeling was nothing more than lust. He was expected to marry a woman of royal blood, not a street-smart American who didn't officially exist even in her own country.

He returned the covers to their place over the fitted sheet and dropped the pillow onto the bed. Turning, he searched his apartment. He already knew that it was empty. The silence was almost suffocating.

His clothes, once scattered on the foyer floor, were now stacked on the table. Her clothing was gone. A folded piece of white paper lay on top of his clothes. He picked it up, scanned the contents, and felt rage, not at her, but at his failure to keep her wrapped firmly in his arms. He slowly exhaled a breath and shook his head in wary amusement as he read it again.

Hugs. Didn't want to wake you after a fabulous night. Had to go to work. Call when I can—don't own a phone.
A.

A messy heart had been drawn before her initial. Closing his eyes, he resisted the urge to crush the note in his hand. His lovers never left him. It had always been the other way around. Everything about Aimee left him feeling off-kilter. He opened his eyes and pursed his lips into a determined line. It was time to change that.

He had kissed every single one of her battle scars last night. If he were a religious man, he would have thanked whatever god there was above for watching over her until he found her. She should have been dead a dozen times if half the tales she shared were true—and he believed they were from the evidence marring her beautiful skin.

"No longer, Aimee. You will be pampered and protected," he vowed, gathering his clothes and turning on his heel.

"You want to do what?!" Tarek exclaimed in disbelief.

"I want to take Aimee back to Jawahir."

Tarek raised his eyebrows. "You never take your mistresses home. I'm *assuming* from the photo on the front page of every major newspaper in the world today that this 'Aimee' is your mistress now," he said, tossing a half dozen newspapers on the coffee table.

On the front page of each was a photo of him bending Aimee back for a passionate kiss at the gala. He scowled as he thumbed through each edition and saw the headline from Jawahir's major news organization: *Has the Heir of Jawahir finally found his Chosen?* While he didn't care that his picture was on the front page, he wasn't sure how Aimee would feel.

"Father woke me this morning and wanted to know if you had lost your mind," Tarek dryly inquired.

"I have," Qadir absently replied.

Tarek's chuckle made him ruefully shrug. "I have to find her, Tarek. I have to get her to Jawahir before something happens to her."

Tarek frowned. "Is she in danger?"

Qadir threw his hands up in the air and walked over to the bank of windows that overlooked Central Park. He should have taken her to his manor house just outside of the city. She wouldn't have been able to escape him nearly as easily there.

Who am I kidding? She probably would have waltzed out the front gate and my guards would have been oblivious! he silently groused.

"She is a danger to herself. She has been shot, stabbed, fallen from buildings, hit by cars… the list goes on," he growled in frustration.

Tarek grimaced. "Are you sure she is the one you want, Qadir? What about Lydia St. Michaels? Surely you could find someone to entertain you that doesn't have a death wish."

Qadir glared at his brother over his shoulder. "No."

Tarek sighed. "Now that I have a first name… it will help in finding her. You didn't perchance get her address, phone number, or Social Security number?" he asked with a raised eyebrow.

"No address, she doesn't have a phone, and no," he admitted.

"She doesn't have a cell phone? In this day and age, what type of person doesn't have a cell phone?"

Qadir chuckled. "An intriguing woman named Aimee Wheels," he murmured.

Bert Crank and Anderson Coldhouse watched Becker's Courier Service from an unmarked car. In the driver's seat, Bert leaned forward and lit a cigarette. Anderson pulled it out of his partner's mouth, lowered the window, and tossed it out.

"Do you fucking want them to see us?" Anderson growled.

"What's got you so worked up? Who the hell cares if anyone sees us?" Bert snapped. "I haven't had a fucking cigarette in hours. My wife has been bitching about how they are going to kill me, and she thinks I've quit. I've been having to sneak them."

Anderson ignored his partner's aggrieved look.

"She's right. Those things'll kill you."

"What are we doing here? You wanting to add Becker to the list?" Bert looked doubtfully at the flow of couriers entering and exiting the building.

SOMETHING ABOUT AIMEE

"Maybe."

"What are we going to get? Their tips? The place is buzzing. There's too much going on," Bert observed.

"I'm not after that." Anderson brooded, his eyes fixed on the front door.

"What are you after then?" Bert asked with cranky exasperation.

Anderson shook his head. "It's need-to-know. Let's go."

Bert grunted in response, and shifted the car into gear. He was about to pull away from the curb when a figure on a skateboard crossed in front of them. She turned her head toward them as she passed, and her vivid, violet eyes bored into Anderson's.

He lifted his hand, curled his fingers to mimic a gun, and depressed his thumb with a cruel smile.

The woman returned his smile with one of her own. She lifted her gloved hand and raised her middle finger.

"Who's that?" Bert asked in a wary voice, watching the woman as she rode down the sidewalk away from Becker's.

"Trouble."

Bert looked in his side mirror. "Want my help?"

"No. No, I'll take care of this one myself. I might need you later, that's all."

Bert shrugged. "Alright then. This has been fun," he muttered.

Anderson didn't respond. There was too much riding on his next move. He wouldn't allow anyone, especially some street rat, to stop him.

Aimee leaned her shoulder against a rough brick wall and watched the unmarked Ford Crown Victoria pull away from the curb, perform an illegal U-turn, and accelerate in the opposite direction. She grimaced when an oncoming car screeched to a stop and the driver laid on the horn. The sound ricocheted off the surrounding buildings.

Frowning, she considered the possibility that Coldhouse had been here for her, but she figured she didn't rate high enough in his estimation to be on his radar. Tucking her skateboard under her arm, she slowly walked back toward Stanley's place, contemplating what their surveillance could have been about.

She stopped at the corner and studied the building. It made little sense for Coldhouse to try to shake down Stanley. Ninety percent of Stanley's income came from contracts or credit cards, not cash. There were also too many employees. Coldhouse preyed on the small mom-and-pop places—specifically immigrant owners in poor neighborhoods.

A well-established upper middle-class white dude in a good business district was definitely off-limits.

"So, what's he up to?" she wondered out loud.

There was nothing else to do, she decided. She would ask Stanley. If she didn't like the answers she got from him, she would ask her feelers on the streets, the ones who had eyes and ears in the NYPD.

She cut around to the side entrance and entered the building. Peter was picking up his next batch of deliveries. The workroom was empty. All the others were still out.

"Wheels, get your ass in here," Stanley yelled.

Peter gave her a sympathetic smile as he pushed his bike past her. "He's been like a bear with a sore tooth all morning."

"Got it."

"Get your ass out of here, Peter, or you'll be on-call this weekend," Stanley growled.

"I'm going, old man. Keep your tighty-whities from bunching up," Peter retorted.

"I don't wear old man underwear!"

Aimee laughed, and Peter, deciding not to test Stanley further, disappeared. Aimee walked over and rested her arms on the counter.

"So, what kind of underwear do you wear? Or do you not wear any at all?" she teased with one of her best grins.

Stanley flushed and shook his head. "You've been around the others too long," he complained.

Aimee laughed and pulled her scanner out. "I need to charge this," she said.

Stanley took her scanner and plugged it in. She waited for him to give her another one and raised an eyebrow when he didn't. He flushed a little redder, and placed a copy of the New York Centennial on the counter along with more than a dozen post-it notes—all with the same number written on them with the words 'call me' in big, fat letters.

She picked up the newspaper, opened it, and grinned. "Cinderella could have learned a thing or two from me," she commented, admiring the photo. "Damn, he's a great kisser," she said with a dreamy sigh.

Stanley cleared his throat. "Yeah, well, tell Cinderella to get her own damn answering service! I'm trying to run a business here, not answer calls from Prince Charming," he complained without heat. In fact, his expression was a little concerned.

Aimee fingered the post-it notes, then covered Stanley's hand with hers.

"What's bothering you, Stanley?"

"I worry about you, Wheels. You have too big a heart, and I'm afraid it's going to get shattered into a million pieces."

The sincerity in his voice brought tears to Aimee's eyes. She squeezed his hand in comfort.

"I'm a lot tougher than you realize, Stanley."

He shook his head. "You've never been in love, little girl. This guy—" Stanley tapped the photo. "This guy isn't like Carl or Peter or any of the other guys you've met. This one takes innocent little girls and crushes their dreams for fun. You're like a wild bird, Wheels. Men like him cage them to show them off, then replace them when they get tired of them or when…" he trailed into a whisper, "when they die."

It was at that moment that Aimee realized Stanley was speaking from experience. She studied the photo of herself and Qadir locked in a passionate kiss, and she tried to see it through Stanley's eyes. She saw the power that Qadir emitted—the danger and the strength. But, she also noted the way he held her protectively in his arms.

She remembered the relief and pleasure in his eyes when he noticed her arrival and the way he had looked at her with so much desire when she took off her cloak. The best part was the shudder that ran through his body when they kissed as if he had been a man on the verge of death who had been given life-saving water.

"Who was she?" Aimee asked, not looking up at Stanley.

"My youngest daughter. She was only eighteen when she met Douglas at a party. He was the son of a wealthy son-of-a-bitch. He was arrogant, spoiled, and impulsive. He promised Chrissy the moon, took everything she offered, and left her crushed when he grew tired of her," he said in a rough voice.

Aimee looked up at him. There were tears in his eyes. Her heart broke for this proud man who had opened his heart and his business to a bunch of misfits and cared about each one of them as if they were his own kids.

"What happened to her?" she asked, afraid that she already knew what kind of ending this story had.

Stanley wiped his eyes. "She died from complications during the birth of our grandson. He lived two hours before he passed as well," he said, taking a loud, shaky breath.

"And Douglas?"

Stanley shook his head. "He had a sudden desire to go abroad. His father offered a nice little sympathy package if we kept our mouths shut about the whole sordid affair."

Aimee squeezed his hand. "What'd you tell him to do with that?"

Stanley snorted. "I told him to shove his money up his arrogant ass. The kid was busted in some foreign country for doing drugs and partying with the wrong woman. He spent five years rotting in a prison his daddy couldn't bribe him out of. Last I heard, he's been in and out of rehab."

"Qadir isn't like that, Stanley—and I'm not Chrissy. I know what the rules are. I don't have dreams of someone like Qadir—well, I do, but they are realistic. We're from two different worlds. He lives in penthouses and palaces. I live—well, let's just say my home is a touch more modest, but that doesn't mean I can't create memories," she gently told him.

"You just be careful, girl. I'm not the only one who will kick his royal ass if he hurts you," Stanley affectionately warned.

Aimee laughed, leaned over the counter, and kissed Stanley's weathered cheek. "I'll help hold him down if he does," she promised. "Now, I need to ask you something important, and I need you to be honest with me."

Eight

Qadir ran a tired hand over his eyes as he tried to focus on the paperwork in front of him. He had been reading the same document for the past five minutes. He would not be able to tell his Secretary of Natural Resources a thing about what he was supposed to have read. His phone vibrated and he answered it with an irritated growl.

"I will call you once I have finished reading over the proposal," he snapped.

"Well, since you said that so cheerfully, I might have to make you a more enticing offer," Aimee teased.

He swiveled around in his chair and stood up, looking out over the cityscape. He gripped the phone tighter and breathed a silent prayer of relief. She was out there somewhere.

"Where are you?" he demanded.

Her amused laughter sounded like music to his ear. "How about starting with 'Hi, Aimee. I'm so glad you called. Did you have a lovely day? How about I meet you for dinner? I know you must be starving.'"

His lips curved into a rueful smile. Shaking his head, he closed his eyes and sighed.

"Hello, Aimee. I'm thrilled that you finally called me. I'm glad you did not kill yourself today. Where can I pick you up so I can take you to dinner?"

"I've got the perfect place," she replied from behind him.

Qadir stiffened in surprise and turned toward the door of his office. Aimee was standing there, leaning against the doorframe. She disconnected the call, and they both lowered their cell phones.

Her hair was in a long braid over her right shoulder. She was wearing her old coat and a pair of blue jeans with a long rip across each thigh. Under the material, he could see she was wearing black leggings. Her jeans were tucked into a pair of knee-high brown boots, and she was looking at him with the soft, teasing expression that made his heart swell. He knew he was staring at her, but he didn't care. To him, she was the most beautiful woman in the world.

He slowly walked around his desk. They met in the center of his office. He cupped her buttocks and lifted her. She wrapped her legs around his waist and locked her ankles together as their lips connected.

Her hands were splayed across the back of his head and the tip of her tongue teased his. He groaned when she threaded her fingers through his hair.

"I missed you," she confessed, pressing tiny kisses all over his face.

"Why didn't you call sooner?"

She captured his lips again. Qadir turned and sat her on the edge of his desk so he could run his hands over her. She pulled him closer so his crotch was pressed firmly against hers.

"This office doesn't by any chance come equipped with a bed, does it?" she breathlessly asked, tilting her head back so he could reach her neck.

"No. We'll have to improvise," he said, unfastening his trousers.

Thirty minutes later, Aimee gave herself a critical look in the bathroom mirror. Her lips were swollen, and she glowed. She felt like she could fly and her body hummed with contentment.

She grimaced as she pulled her sweater away from her tender breasts. She might need to wear a bra for some padded protection if Qadir kept giving them the attention he did. The thought made her smile. It was a price she was willing to pay.

The door opened, and in the mirror, she saw Qadir leaning against the doorframe. He might not have the soft, glowing aura around him, but he did look like a well-satisfied man. He held up her coat, and she slipped her arms into it. A shiver of delight and desire cascaded through her when he kissed her neck, just below her left ear, as he adjusted her collar.

"You are beautiful, *habibi*," he murmured, wrapping his arms around her waist and pulling her back against him.

She tilted her head and accepted his kiss. Lifting her hand, she caressed his cheek. She had fallen for him fast. The thought should have scared the hell out of her, but it didn't. Considering her unusual upbringing, it was an emotion she never thought that she would experience. Still, like everything else in life, she embraced it as a treasure to be captured, admired, and enjoyed to the fullest, even knowing that she might have to let it go one day.

"I'm falling in love with you, Qadir." She looked at his expression in the mirror when she said it.

The pleased smile on his lips made her heart skip a beat, but it was the expression in his eyes that made her relax in his embrace. He might not want to admit it yet, maybe he didn't even realize it yet, but he was falling in love with her too.

"You should let me purchase you new clothes," he said.

She laughed and shook her head. "I've got as many as my closet can hold. I'm starving. How about I take you out tonight? Well, you and your bodyguards," she teased.

"When did you get a cell phone?"

Aimee twisted in his arms and kissed him. "Today. It is one of those disposable ones, but it works. I didn't realize that since cell phones have taken over, there are very few public phone booths anymore—at least ones that work. Now, how about some food?"

"I am your humble guest this evening."

"You… humble?" She snorted.

"I can be," he defended with a wicked look in his eyes.

"Let's put that to the test," she said.

An hour later, Aimee guided the entourage, including Qadir's brother, Tarek, who she hadn't been properly introduced to until now, toward a nondescript building in the not-so-nice section of Harlem. She had convinced a very reluctant Qadir and Tarek to trust her about not bringing their own vehicles. Instead, she made them call a ride-service. It took three cars to transport the group to the club.

"What is this place?" Tarek asked, looking up at the graffiti-covered building.

"It's a legit place. Come on, you might actually enjoy it," she teased.

Buddy, the black bouncer, grinned at her, then caught sight of her six well-dressed companions and scowled. Aimee smiled, and Buddy scrutinized each man, shaking his head.

"No heat inside. You'll have to check in your weapons," Buddy stated.

"I already warned them, Bud."

"You okay, Wheels?" he asked.

"Yeah, I'm gonna have a really great night. Is Idella here tonight?"

Buddy nodded. "Yeah." He tilted his head toward the interior as he opened the door.

Aimee led the men inside. She sensed their startled reactions when they entered. They were expecting this place to be a rundown shithole. Instead, it was like stepping back in time to the glamorous 1920s.

The sound of a jazz band and a woman's deep, sultry singing voice washed over them, sending a shiver down Aimee's spine.

Idella opened the nightclub she called *Colours* five years ago, converting the old warehouse into a spectacular music symposium with the help of the community she had grown up with. Some of the best chefs in New York worked here, and the singers and musicians were unforgettable.

Idella had a dream of creating the next Greenwich Village for artists. Local musicians mixed with artists from around the world. Aimee guided the men over to the clerk who took their weapons, placing them in the lockers behind her and giving them a ticket. Tarek grumbled under his breath. Aimee patted his arm.

"It's better than sitting in a cold car for hours. The food will make you feel better," she promised.

"Ms. Aimee, if you and your party will follow me," a waitress dressed in a 1920s Flapper dress politely suggested.

Aimee threaded her arm through Qadir's and smiled at him. "Maybe we'll actually get to dance this time," she said.

She paused at the entrance, allowing the full effect of Idella's creation to sink in. The interior of the building had been modernized with all the required safety codes, but artfully concealed to hide it. Chandeliers made from recycled glass by a local artist hung from the ceiling.

There were three levels inside. On the ground floor, there were dozens of tables that surrounded a massive dance floor. The second level was for fine dining, while the third level contained Idella's personal residence, offices, and apartments for the traveling musicians.

They followed the waitress up the wide staircase to the second floor.

"Who is that?" Tarek asked, staring at the singer on the stage below them.

"That's Idella. She owns this place."

The waitress directed the bodyguards to a table covered with a pristine white tablecloth edged with silver and guided Aimee, Qadir, and Tarek to another. Flickering in the center of each table was a trio of tea-light candles ensconced in beautiful stained-glass candelabras.

The waitress handed them menus and recited the night's house special before taking their drink orders. Aimee sighed and leaned her chin in her palm. She already knew what she wanted—the Lemon Chicken with the delicate sauce, side of pasta, and fresh vegetables. This was one of her favorite treats.

"I can see why you love it here," Qadir said, placing his arm across the back of her chair.

Aimee nodded. "Idella has done so much for this community. She was gifted with an incredible voice, and she knows how to wield the power of it."

"Idella... that is *the* Idella?" Tarek asked, his gaze locked on the tall, slender woman with chestnut-colored skin in a shimmering silver gown.

"Yes. Isn't she amazing?" Aimee replied with a serene smile on her lips.

Aimee had surprised him again. He didn't know why. She was an incredible woman with so many layers that he knew it would take him a lifetime to uncover them all. She had told him very little about her life, but the small glimpses he caught were tantalizing.

The meal, performances, and service were outstanding. A different band had taken over the stage and was playing a series of slow, romantic songs. They walked down the stairs to the dance floor. Qadir held her close to him, savoring the feel of her in his arms.

"I have to leave tomorrow," he murmured near her ear. "There are matters at home that I must take care of. I want you to come with me."

She stiffened. They turned in a tight circle, moving with the other dancers, and she tightened her grip on his shoulders before deliberately relaxing against him.

"I can't, but thank you. How long will you be gone?"

"If you do not go with me, a week at the most. Why can't you go?"

She rubbed her cheek against him. "I have responsibilities here. I'll be here when you get back," she promised.

"You don't have to work, Aimee," he said.

She leaned back and placed her fingers against his lips. "Don't spoil what we have, Qadir."

Frustration burned inside him, but he was afraid that if he pushed his elusive bird too hard, she would disappear. He cupped her hand and twirled her around. When the song ended, she led him in a different direction than their table. He glanced back and saw his brother talking to the lovely and talented Idella.

"Where are we going?" he asked.

"I want to show you something," she said.

They stepped into an old freight elevator and exited on the third floor. Aimee led him along the corridor. Looking over the hallway's railing to the club below, Qadir was once again impressed with the night club. The band had taken a break and a group of thespians were performing a short skit.

The diversity in the audience was clear, spanning from some of the wealthiest patrons in the world to a variety of local residents. The club was a bridge where all came to be entertained. He was astonished that he had never heard of the club before. He started walking again when Aimee gently tugged on his hand.

They passed through a door and up a series of stairs to the roof. At the top, a glass atrium filled with plants, furniture, and water features overlooked the neighborhood. Aimee released his hand and walked over to appreciate the horizon.

"Isn't it beautiful?" she asked.

Qadir looked at the glow of the city and made a vague, noncommittal sound as he stepped close behind her. She leaned back against his chest, and he enfolded her in his arms.

"The city is its own kind of desert, I suppose, though its beauty doesn't call to me. All the same, this is a wonderful oasis, Aimee. Thank you for bringing me here."

"You're welcome." She smiled, warmed all the way through that he liked her surprise date.

"Tell me more about you. Tell me about your life. I want to know everything."

Aimee paused. *Well,* she thought, *might as well start from the beginning.* She smiled ruefully.

"Yolanda, my adopted mom, found me behind a dumpster when I was a few hours old," she began.

Qadir started at the news. Shock and horror held him still.

Aimee chuckled sadly. "Yolanda was my mom, my mentor, and had a heart of gold. Winter came early twenty-one years ago, and Yolanda happened down that alley at just the right moment."

"What day?" he asked.

"November 1st, Día de los Muertos, the Day of the Dead." Aimee grinned.

"Yolanda said that I must have had ancestors watching over me. She believed in those things—as well as a bunch of other superstitions. No one ever questioned how a young black woman came to have a white daughter."

She looked down at their joined hands and rubbed her thumb against his darker skin. "I don't think I ever fully appreciated all the things she did for me. The first five years, she moved from place to place, staying one step ahead of child services. She told me that they didn't know nothing about raising a baby. They would have stuck me in some home where the people would have tried to box in my free spirit instead of letting me fly.

"I never attended a proper school. Technically, I didn't exist. There was no birth certificate. She took me to local clinics when I needed my shots or was sick. It wasn't until I went through her things after she died that I discovered she used her daughter's information to get what I needed."

"What happened to her daughter?" he asked.

"Social Services took her before Yolanda ever got to see her. Yolanda was raised in the system. She fell in love with a young gang member who was murdered in a drive-by shooting. Shortly after his death, she discovered she was pregnant with his child. She was sixteen when she had her daughter, Aimee Raine Wheels. After she turned eighteen, she tried to get custody of her daughter. She had been working, going to school, and she rented a small apartment. She did everything right, only to discover that her daughter had been killed when she was six months old. It was the foster mother's boyfriend who did it. Yolanda went a little crazy until she found me. She swore that she would protect me and teach me everything I needed to know so no one could ever hurt me." Aimee absently wiped her damp cheek.

Qadir held her close and stroked her cheek. "I'm so sorry, Aimee. I don't know what to say."

"It wasn't all bad. There was a lot of love in our lives. We had each other, and she taught me to embrace the wild craziness of the people we knew. I'm fluent in eight languages. I kept learning more so I could talk to more people. She took me to the library every day that it was open. She didn't have a library card and would stuff books under her clothes or rummage through the trash bin for any books the library tossed out. The old cart she pulled around was always full of books that we would read over and over. We learned and grew together. Her favorites were fairy tales: the Arabian Nights and King Arthur and the Knights of the Round Table. She promised that one day we would travel the world, dip our toes in the Mediterranean, slide down the side of a sand dune, ride a camel, climb to the top of the Eiffel Tower, yell out our names at the Grand Canyon, and so many more adventures."

"But you never did," he concluded, feeling her pain as if it were his own.

She leaned her head back. "Only in books," she said with a sigh.

"What happened to her?"

"I was sixteen when she started losing weight and having bad headaches—the kind that made her cry and pass out. She never had much weight to spare, anyway. I finally made her go to the hospital. They diagnosed her with brain cancer. She was gone six weeks later. I felt like the sun died that day," she said, tears streaming down her cheeks. "I claimed her ashes and took them down to the river. It wasn't the Mediterranean, and it wasn't warm, but it was as close as we could get to dipping our toes in the water."

Qadir turned her in his arms and rubbed his chin against the top of her head. She held him as if she would never let him go, and he hoped she never did.

"I could take you to Paris and to the Mediterranean, and all the other places in your books," he said.

She gave a watery laugh, leaned back, and wiped the tears from her face. "That sounds good, but not tomorrow. Stanley needs all the help he can get at the moment, and I'm not about to jump ship right before the holiday season. We'll talk more when you get back from your trip," she promised.

Later that night, Qadir stared up at the ceiling with Aimee tucked securely against his side. He was used to taking what he wanted—or buying it, but nothing he did could convince Aimee to come with him. She had finally admitted that without a birth certificate or driver's license, it was impossible for her to get a passport.

"Let me work on getting my ID and stuff," she had said.

Her life was much like the tribes of nomads in the various wild places of Jawahir. He caressed her side. Her bare leg stroked his in her sleep. They fit perfectly together.

Fatigue pulled on him. There was much to be done. He would call in a few favors from his contacts in Washington, D.C. and get her documents expedited. He needed to prepare his father, King Melik Saif-Ad-Din, for the inevitable union between himself and Aimee. He would not accept another as his bride.

Qadir closed his eyes and smiled at the thought of taking Aimee to all the places she dreamed about. He held her hand. Soon, they would sleep together like this all the time.

It wasn't until he was almost asleep that he realized that he still didn't know where Aimee lived.

Nine

Qadir stared out of the window of the limousine. Tarek was unusually quiet as well. The drizzle of rain fit his mood. He had woken alone again.

He turned his head to face his brother. "Tarek, will you do me a favor, please?"

Tarek blinked and nodded. "Anything, Qadir."

"Will you find someone to follow Aimee? I need to know where she goes, who she sees, and most of all, where she lives."

Tarek frowned. "Do you suspect she is cheating on you?"

Qadir scowled and shook his head. "No. I worry about her. She refuses to accept anything from me, not even a cell phone. I want to make sure she is safe. That is all."

Tarek smiled in understanding. "Consider it done."

Qadir nodded his thanks and returned to his view of the gray, wet concrete and looming dark buildings. The week away from Aimee was going to seem like an eternity. The morning already did.

Aimee was shivering with cold. On her last delivery, a car had driven past her and splashed cold water up her legs. She chatted a little with Mrs. Yang, then placed her shopping basket on the floor near the cat food, headed to the back of the Yangs' grocery store, and closed the bathroom door behind her.

After removing her boots and stripping out of her wet jeans, she turned on the hand dryer and held her jeans under it, hoping to dry her pants and warm her hands at the same time. It was hard not to crawl up under the dryer and just stay there. If it wasn't for the seven hungry mouths she had to feed, she would have seriously considered it—though the resulting electric bill and hogged bathroom would not endear her to the Yangs… so, probably not. A girl could dream.

Ten minutes later, her jeans were still damp but no longer dripping and warmer than they had been. She dressed and opened the bathroom door. Across the hall, the office door was open, and she could see the video feed from a store security camera that Mr. Yang must have installed recently.

She walked down the short hall and retrieved her basket, adding two dozen cans of cat food to it, a loaf of bread, a jar of peanut butter, and two containers of noodle soup. She was off work for the next two days and the forecast called for more rain.

She picked up a package of cough drops as well. Her throat had been feeling scratchy since around noon. The last thing she needed was to get sick.

She walked up to the register just as two teenage boys entered the store. She recognized them as members of a local gang. Mr. Yang came out of the back to ring her up while Mrs. Yang headed for the back office, the two of them seamlessly moving to their usual positions when someone dangerous came into the store.

"Yo, nice board," one of the boys said, eyeing the skateboard she had propped up next to her.

She ignored him, smiling at Mr. Yang as she bought the food and packed it all into her bag. The boy started to reach for her skateboard, but she caught it with her foot, sliding it between herself and the counter. She adjusted her bag on her shoulder.

"What's the matter? You don't want to share your board?"

"Thank you, Mr. Yang," she said in Mandarin.

"You be careful, Aimee," he replied in the same language.

She grabbed her board and turned to find the teen standing so close that her bulging bag actually hit him. He was glaring at her.

With casual detachment she said, "Tell Biggy that Wheels sends her love and that I'll stop by to see his grandma this week."

The suddenly wary boy stepped back. The second boy snickered and lightly punched him in the arm. She stood still while the skateboard-lover looked her up and down.

"You know Biggy?" he grudgingly asked.

Aimee stared back at him, not smiling. "Yes. The Yangs are under my protection. Biggy promised me five places. This is one of them."

"You're full of shit. Why would Biggy give you grace?"

Aimee did smile then. It didn't reach her eyes.

"Why don't you ask Biggy?" she suggested.

She pushed past the boy and pulled open the door. Adjusting the hood on her coat, she entered the rain-darkened night. She didn't look behind her when the bell jingled again as someone left the store behind her.

"She's still not answering her phone," Qadir growled, pocketing his cell phone as he exited the small private jet.

"The man I have following Aimee is concerned about her," Tarek replied as they walked to the car.

They slid into the limousine, and Tarek handed Qadir the report. He flicked through it with a frown. Aimee had gone into an abandoned warehouse three days ago and hadn't come out.

"We'll be there in about forty-five minutes. The realtor will let us in," Tarek informed him.

Qadir looked out the window. A storm had passed through this area nearly two days ago. Six inches of snow remained on the ground. Pedestrians, bundled up against the bone-chilling cold, carefully avoided the mounds of dirty snow the city workers had piled up along the curbs. It was a dramatic difference from where he was yesterday.

Forty-five minutes later, they pulled up outside of the abandoned warehouse. A tall chain-link fence surrounded the building down to the edge of the water. A large For Sale sign was posted on the gate.

Qadir studied the building for several minutes before a Kia SUV pulled up, and a woman in her fifties wearing heavy make-up and a suit that was too snug for her size hurried over. Her blood-red painted lips were plastered in a large smile. Greed and appreciation gleamed in her eyes. At her approach, he powered down his window.

One of his bodyguards stopped her before she could reach the limo. A mild argument ensued before she handed the man the keys to the gate and another set for the warehouse. She gave a plaintive look at the limo before retreating to the warmth of her car.

The keys were quickly used to open the gate, they drove to the entrance, and all but the drivers exited the cars and approached the front door. Qadir's bodyguard unlocked it.

The man who had been tailing Aimee stepped out of the gloom. Qadir and Tarek nodded to him, and they all entered the freezing tomb of what was once a prime manufacturing building.

Each of them turned on their powerful flashlights and swept beams of light around the neglected interior. The warehouse was nearly the length of a football field. Their breath fogged the air. Their footsteps echoed.

"Where did she enter?" Qadir asked.

The man who had followed Aimee replied, "Over there, sir."

Qadir walked over to the spot on the far side of the warehouse. Beneath a window, a wooden box displayed many dirty footprints, all in the same shoe size, some faint, some newer. He followed the tracks.

They were almost to the stairs when a movement out of the darkness set his bodyguards on alert. Qadir relaxed when several kittens appeared. Within moments, six kittens and a mother cat wound around their legs meowing loudly.

Tarek's beam of light illuminated empty cat food cans neatly clustered on the floor and piled in a trash bin nearby.

"Someone's been feeding them," Tarek noted.

Qadir nodded, looking up at the top of the stairs. A closed office door was visible.

A muffled cough spurred Qadir to take the stairs two at a time and push open the door. Tarek was right behind him.

He shone the flashlight around the room. A small stove was set up on the table. Another muffled cough and a low moan drew both men's attention to a pile of clothes and blankets. A shiver of dread ran through Qadir. His heart wanted to reject what his mind understood. Crossing the small room, he knelt down next to the makeshift bed and slowly pulled the covers back.

"Aimee, *habibi*, what have you done?"

He pulled his glove off and caressed her flushed cheek. She was burning up!

Her eyelashes fluttered, and she gave him a crooked smile before wincing and burying her face in the covers as a prolonged coughing fit gripped her.

"Qadir," Tarek murmured beside him.

"Call Dr. Fuah. Have him meet us at the hospital," he said.

"No... no... hos-hospital," Aimee pleaded.

"This time I will have to overrule you, *habibi*."

"Not-not moving. Too c-c-cold," she grumbled, trying to pull the covers back over her head.

"Aimee," he growled.

She shook her head before wearily closing her eyes. "C-can you pl-please feed-feed the kit-kit-kittens?"

"Get her out of here," Tarek gently ordered. "Dr. Fuah will meet you at the manor house. He says the hospitals are swamped at the moment. If she needs more care, he will have her transferred to a private hospital."

"I'll take care of the kittens for the Miss," the man who had been following her said.

Qadir ignored them all. He threw aside the pile of clothes on top of Aimee, wrapped the quilt around her, and scooped her into his arms. She briefly struggled as he stepped through the door.

"My stuff! I need it. My board. I—" She coughed. "—got to have... my board." She turned her head into the covers as she coughed again.

"Go," Tarek said. "I'll gather her belongings and bring them."

Qadir shot his brother an expression of gratitude before he carried Aimee down the stairs. He strode toward the entrance, his mind still reeling from the fact that his lover lived as a homeless person while he traveled in luxury.

He slid into the back seat of the limousine. The driver immediately pulled away. They exited the gate without stopping for the realtor who had eagerly opened her door hoping to catch him.

As the limo sped through the streets, Qadir held Aimee's shivering body tightly against him. He reached along the door and increased the heat in the confined space. She snuggled against him with a soft sigh.

He looked out at the crowded streets. He felt like he was actually seeing the people walking along the sidewalks for the first time. He had been born into wealth and had never known deprivation. He never worried that his resources were too few to care for himself. He'd certainly never been close to dying from neglect.

How many others were like Aimee; vibrant and capable, but just one unlucky moment away from complete disaster?

Forty minutes later, he was carrying Aimee into his manor house. The butler greeted them at the door. Dr. Fuah and his two nurses followed them in. Qadir ascended the stairs and strode to his master bedroom. The nurses moved ahead of him and turned back the covers. He gently laid Aimee on his bed. She moaned softly, gripped the covers of her worn quilt, and rolled onto her side and curled into a ball.

"I will inform you of her condition, sire," Dr. Fuah said with a stern expression.

Qadir wanted to argue but bowed his head in agreement. He quietly exited the room as the two nurses began talking soothingly to Aimee.

He walked into the living room and stopped, unsure of what to do. He had never felt so helpless in his life.

Walking over to the bar, he poured a drink of bourbon. He looked up when Tarek entered carrying Aimee's scant belongings.

"This is everything," Tarek said, placing the small collection of items next to the couch. "Bill will capture the cats. He said between his wife and daughter, they will have a good home."

"Thank you, Tarek," he said.

Tarek looked up. "Any word on her condition?"

Qadir shook his head. "Not yet. We've only just arrived ourselves."

Tarek nodded, walked over to the bar and poured himself a drink, then settled onto the couch. Qadir sighed and sat down in the chair across from him. He stretched his long legs out in front of himself and stared at the golden liquor in his glass without actually seeing it. All he could see was Aimee's flushed face. All he could hear were her brutal coughs.

"You are falling in love with her," Tarek commented.

Qadir smiled. "Not falling—have fallen," he confessed. He took a deep breath. "She is smart, beautiful, funny, passionate, and she scares the hell out of me."

"Sounds like you won't be bored," Tarek chuckled before shaking his head. "I can't believe she was living there."

Qadir scowled and rose to his feet. "I can't either. If she had told me she was homeless—" He shook his head. "I should have known. Her clothes, her unwillingness to tell me where she lived. She's proud, Tarek, and stubborn. She's independent as hell."

"And compassionate.... She will be a great queen one day."

Qadir bowed his head in agreement. "Yes, she will be."

Time passed slowly. Minutes turned to an hour, then two. Qadir and Tarek talked about the business and politics of their various meetings, but Qadir's eyes kept straying to the doorway. He was about to say to hell with it and go back upstairs when Dr. Fuah appeared.

"Sire," Dr. Fuah said with a bow.

"How is she?"

"She will be fine. She was dehydrated and as far as I can tell without an X-ray, she has pleurisy and mild bronchitis. I have her on an IV drip with antibiotics. She needs nourishment and rest for the next week. I would like the two nurses to remain with her. I'll stop by again tomorrow to check on her."

"Thank you, Dr. Fuah," Qadir replied.

"I'll walk out with you, Kamil," Tarek said.

Dr. Fuah smiled and bowed his head. Qadir waited until they left before he set his glass down on the bar, exited the living room, and took the stairs up to his bedroom two at a time. The two nurses rose to their feet and bowed to him when he entered the room. His eyes were focused on Aimee's pale face.

"How is she?" he inquired.

"We have bathed her, and she is sleeping better. The medicine is already beginning to help, though it will take forty-eight to seventy-two hours before she feels much better."

"There are two bedrooms down the hall. You may use those. I will stay with her tonight," he said.

Both women's eyes widened.

"But sire, we were instructed—"

He gave them a look that had them hastily bowing and exiting the room. The soft click of the door behind him signaled that he was alone with Aimee. He walked over and sat on the edge of the bed, lifting her pale hand in his.

He traced the veins along her skin, and paused, his hand hovering above the IV port. She coughed in her sleep, struggling for a moment to catch her breath, before she settled with a soft sigh.

"Ah, *habibi*, what am I going to do with you?"

Her fingers flexed, squeezing his with the barest of pressure. It was probably wishful thinking, but at the moment, he would take any sign that she heard him. He rose to his feet and went into the bathroom. After a quick shower, he pulled on a pair of jogging pants.

Leaving one of the lights in the bathroom on, he partially closed the door, turned off the bedside table lamp, and crawled into bed. He slid his arm around Aimee. She immediately turned onto her side with her back to him and scooted close. He cushioned her arm so she wouldn't pull on the IV line.

"Qadir," Aimee murmured.

"Yes, *habibi*."

"I'm glad you came back," she mumbled.

He kissed her shoulder. "So am I, *habibi*. So am I."

Ten

Three days later, Qadir was standing in the doorway of his bedroom with his mouth hanging open in disbelief. Aimee was chatting up a storm—in fluent Arabic—with Dr. Fuah and the two nurses. Her face was still pale, and she was still coughing, but her eyes held the sparkle of mischief he had become accustomed to.

"You should rest," Dr. Fuah was saying.

Aimee waved her hand. "I'll be sitting at the desk taking messages and pushing papers. Stanley needs help. It isn't like I'll be busting my board."

"What is going on?" he demanded.

"I was advising Ms. Wheels—" Dr. Fuah began.

"I was just telling the Doc that I'm fine, and I'm grateful for all their wonderful care," Aimee said.

"In perfect Arabic," Qadir observed with a raised eyebrow.

Aimee grinned and shrugged. "It's amazing what you can learn living on the streets."

"You will not be going back to work," Qadir stated. "You need your rest. Three days ago, you were on death's door."

Aimee wiggled her nose at him but wisely kept her mouth shut.

He turned his attention to Dr. Fuah, who was eyeing him and Aimee with a small bemused smile. He motioned for Dr. Fuah to follow him.

Once they were in his living room, he turned to his personal physician with a raised eyebrow. Dr. Fuah smiled again and shook his head. He could tell the man was struggling to form the words he wanted to say. Qadir sighed and raised his hand.

"I find it easier when dealing with Aimee if you just say whatever you have to say."

Dr. Fuah chuckled and nodded. "She is a very unusual woman, sire. She has reacted well to the antibiotics and your care. Technically, she is well enough to do some light duties, but I fear she... might push that definition."

"Is she well enough to travel?" he asked.

Dr. Fuah frowned. "I would be cautious of that. Traveling can be very exhausting, even if done in luxury. I would feel better if her lungs had a few more days to heal."

"Why am I not surprised that fate seems to be against me protecting her? Exactly how long before you recommend that it is safe for her to travel?"

"A week, sire," Dr. Fuah replied.

"A week it will be." He paused and hesitantly asked, "Is there any... Are there *other* restrictions that I should be concerned about?"

Dr. Fuah tried not to smile. "All I can recommend is rest. The more she gets, sire, the more quickly she will heal."

"Your advice is noted, Dr. Fuah," Qadir dryly replied. "Please express my gratitude to Celine and Lara for their excellent care of Aimee. I will take over now."

"Very well, sire. Until you need my services again," Dr. Fuah said with an amused expression.

"Don't jinx me, please."

Dr. Fuah's chuckle faded as he and Aimee's two nurses left. Qadir went back to his bedroom. His heart skipped a beat when he saw the empty bed. A quick scan of the room showed that Aimee was not here. He was reaching for his phone when the muted sounds of water running and Aimee singing pierced the loud thunder of blood rushing through his head.

Qadir closed his eyes for a moment, breathing deeply to calm his racing heart. He chuckled when Aimee hit a bad note, stopped, and tried again. He began unbuttoning his shirt.

Qadir watched with a frown as Aimee came out of the bedroom the next morning dressed in a pair of her tattered jeans and one of his black cashmere sweaters. She was carrying her dark brown courier bag in one hand and her skateboard in the other.

On the phone, his younger brother by five years asked, "Qadir, did you hear what I said?"

"There must have been a bad connection, Junayd. Can you repeat what you said?"

He twisted around, his eyes following Aimee as she poured herself a cup of coffee and grabbed a Danish. She took a bite, moaned, and grabbed two more pastries from the tray, wrapping them in one of the cloth napkins. He felt pure dread when she tucked her prize into her bag. She peered under the lids of the covered dishes, grabbed a plate, and began filling the fine china with eggs, biscuits, and fresh fruit.

"Let me call you back," he growled. He hung up.

"What are you doing?" he asked.

She gave him an innocent, wide-eyed stare. "Getting breakfast. I'm starving!"

"I meant, why are you dressed?"

She stopped and licked her fingers. He followed the movement with his eyes while the lower half of his body responded to each, delicate lick of her tongue. The memories of what she could do with that tongue weren't helping. When he finally noticed the mischievous expression in her eyes, he almost groaned out loud. She knew exactly what she was doing to him—and she was enjoying every second.

He scowled at her, which just made her expression more devious. She curled the tip of her tongue and made a sucking noise. The groan he was suppressing broke free.

"You are not going out," he said in a strained voice.

"Yes, I am," she laughed.

"No, you are not."

She lifted an eyebrow. "Yes, I am. I promised Stanley that I would sort out the paperwork for the deliveries next week. It's Sunday, so no one will be there but me. I won't be out in the cold or running around. I'll be in a nice warm office all by my lonesome."

"You are supposed to be resting," he argued, folding his arms across his chest.

Aimee rolled her eyes. "I might have been in bed, but I don't think there was much resting going on. It was more like non-stop—"

Qadir captured her words in a kiss. He knew he should feel guilty, but it was hard to feel such a negative emotion when his body was humming with contentment. She hungrily returned his kiss. His cell phone buzzed in his pocket, and they were startled into separating.

He retrieved it and lifted it to his ear. "I told you I would call you back."

"This is too important," Tarek replied in a terse tone.

Qadir frowned. "I thought you were Junayd. What's wrong?"

"There is new information on the two men who attacked you. We need to meet at the Harris Building."

"When?" he asked, looking at Aimee.

"As soon as you can get here—and expect the press. This isn't going to be good."

"I'll be there within the hour," he promised, ending the call.

"Trouble?" Aimee asked, looking up at him.

"The two men who attempted to assassinate me—we have learned more about them," he replied.

Aimee hesitated, then nodded. "That's good. How about you drop me off at Stanley's place and pick me up when you're done?"

He opened his mouth to tell her no, but realized that it would be pointless. She would go anyway. At least if he took her, he knew where she would be. He looked at his watch and sighed.

"Can you be ready to leave in—"

"Now," she said, quickly finishing the last of the eggs on her plate even as she rose from her seat.

He chuckled. "I have never met a woman like you," he confessed.

She wiggled her nose at him. "I know," she said with a laugh.

A quick call to his security staff had the limo waiting for them in the circular drive out front. He followed her to the foyer door of the mansion, pausing to help her with her long coat and to pull on his outer coat. Qadir rubbed Aimee's back as they descended the steps. Frigid air greeted them. The day was another dreary one, and he looked forward to returning to the sun and warmth of his homeland.

He pulled her closer to him. He would give her today to finish her obligations to Stanley. Tarek should have the paperwork for her passport completed by the end of the week. Once he had the documents, he could finally whisk Aimee away to Jawahir and introduce her to his parents.

Aimee slid her hand into his and smiled up at him. His heart swelled with love, and he kissed her before ushering her into the limo. Tonight he would ask her to be his wife.

~

Aimee studied the dreary streets and thought about how to tell Qadir that his 'new information' was actually just the fall guy Anderson Coldhouse had set up. The trouble was that Aimee didn't want to give away Biggy as her source.

Aimee had grown up with Biggy. They had stayed close after his brother was killed in a power dispute and Biggy took his brother's place as the leader of most of the gangs in Harlem.

She might question the lifestyle her friend had chosen, but she never judged. They each made their choices, and they lived by a different set of rules than most of society. She chose to help those less fortunate when she could. Biggy did the same in his own way. Unfortunately, his method of financing his charity projects tended to be illegal, not to mention painful for anyone who didn't follow his rules.

Instead of voicing her thoughts, Aimee asked, "Who is Junayd?"

Qadir turned to her, and she smiled. Sometimes it was nice to pretend that they were just two people in love and everything was simple. As much as she needed to talk about wannabe gangster pawns and corrupt cops, it probably wouldn't hurt to stall just a little.

"My younger brother," he answered.

She looked down at their joined hands. "I didn't realize you had another brother. I thought it was just you and Tarek."

"There is much we still need to learn about each other. I also have twin younger brothers, Junayd and Jameel. They are twenty-five. Junayd is a doctor. Jameel's love is computer engineering."

"What did you study? And Tarek?"

He shrugged. "My degrees were in learning how to run a country. For fun, I studied International Business and spent ten years in the military. Tarek spent the same time in the military. His degrees are in Political Science and Counter Terrorism."

Aimee looked at him with a startled expression. "How old are you? You don't look old enough to have spent ten years in the military!"

He chuckled. "Thirty," he replied.

"I hope I age as well as you do," she said with a sigh.

He lifted her hand to his lips and kissed the back of it. "You'll grow more beautiful the longer my eyes behold you, *'amirati alkhayalia,'* he promised.

The limo pulled up in front of Becker's Courier Service, and Aimee bit her lip. One of Qadir's bodyguards opened the door for her. She turned and kissed Qadir, gazing into his eyes as she pulled back.

"Tell Tarek to dig deeper. Andrew Carthmen isn't the kind of guy to be the brains of an assassination attempt. There's something else going on."

He gripped her hand, preventing her from slipping all the way out of the limo. His eyes narrowed and he studied her face.

"How do you know about Andrew Carthmen?"

"The streets talk if you know how to listen. Tarek isn't the only one who wants to keep you safe," she said with a smile, pulling free of his grasp. "Let me know what you find out."

Qadir glowered. "Keep your cell phone on. I will call you when I'm able to return."

Aimee held her disposable phone up and grinned as she walked away. She could feel Qadir's eyes on her until she rounded the building to the employee entrance.

She breathed in the chilled air. If she finished in time, she could go see the Yangs and visit her old home. There was a special box she'd kept hidden that she wanted to retrieve.

After pressing the code into the keypad, she slipped inside, moved the box for drop-offs with her foot, and closed the door behind her.

Eleven

"I don't know about this, Anderson," Bert grumbled. "The guy you are dealing with makes me nervous. What does he want with Becker?"

Anderson hid his amusement. His dear brother made a lot of people nervous—as they should be. Anderson wished it was his brother backing him up now instead of his annoying partner, but beggars couldn't be choosers. He parked by the curb across the street from Becker's Courier Service.

"What the fuck is really going on? This is bigger than intimidating some mom-and-pop places, isn't it? You've gotten into some hard-core stuff where they don't play around."

"Shut up, Bert."

Bert fell silent, but he didn't stop fidgeting. Irritation flared inside Anderson. If he hadn't needed Bert when he first transferred into the precinct, he would never have chosen the man as his partner—nor recruited him for the lucrative side jobs.

It had been easy to manipulate Bert into helping him thanks to a high-maintenance wife and daughter who drove up enormous credit card bills, but the man's incessant complaining grated on his nerves.

"So, what are we doing here?" Bert asked.

Anderson scowled at the fidgeting man beside him. "Get behind the wheel and stay in the car. I'll let you know if I need you."

"Whatever you say, man," Bert mumbled, opening the passenger door and stepping out.

Anderson exited the driver's door and looked both ways along the empty street. He pulled up the collar of his long overcoat and crossed the road.

If everything worked out, he would be in and out before anyone knew he was there. He stopped by the front entrance and visualized the schematic of the building's interior that he had pulled from the building and code enforcement records. He glanced around one more time to make sure no one was watching.

Removing the casing on the keypad by the front door with the fine edge of his knife, he pulled the red wire loose and touched it to the solenoid. The electronic lock disengaged, and he pulled the door open. A bell chimed. He silently cursed.

He entered the lobby and closed the door behind him. A long counter with a plexiglass shield ran halfway to the ceiling, separating the lobby from the reception area. Behind the counter, a door to the right opened to a lounge area for the employees, and a hallway led to a back office, bathroom, and warehouse.

A large stack of papers in the file tray on the other side of the partition caught his attention. He walked over to the door and twisted the handle. It was locked. It opened outward, so he couldn't kick it in.

Pulling out his knife, he used the tip between the lock and the frame. It popped open, and he walked through the door. He laid the knife down on the counter, picked up the stack of papers, and began sorting through the envelopes.

∼

Down the hallway from the reception room, in the back office, Aimee had been sorting drop-offs for half an hour when she came across a large manila envelope with dark red stains on it. It looked like blood splatter. She was about to add it to Stanley's pile when she saw a familiar name on the front.

H.R.H. Q. Saif-Ad-Din
Urgent

The address was smeared, but Aimee recognized it as Qadir's penthouse address.

Aimee debated opening the envelope. Giving in, she slid the letter opener along the top, removed the contents, and stared in shock and horror at the photos of dead men, women, and children lined up in rows. Men in military gear stood over them. Her hand shook as she read the names and descriptions written in Arabic at the bottom of each photo. A close-up photo showed who was in command, and his name was written at the bottom of the photo, too.

The name was frighteningly familiar.

Aimee pulled her cell phone out of her pocket, turned the camera on, and took a photo of each graphic picture. Tears burned her eyes when she turned to the last one and saw the map of Jawahir with three small circles on it.

She was about to take a photo of the map when the front door chimed. She looked up with a frown. No one should have entered through the front door—not today, anyway.

She rose from her chair, stuffing all the photos except for the map back into the envelope while silently cursing Stanley for not replacing the broken CCTV security system. She folded the map and slid it into her back pocket to study later.

On the cell phone, she switched the camera to video mode. After turning off the overhead light, she quietly opened the door. She held the phone in front of her as she exited the office, sliding along the scuffed brown wood-paneled wall of the dark hallway until she could see who was in the lobby.

All she could tell was that whoever it was, they were tall. Fortunately, the door between the reception area and the lobby was locked. That sense of relief faded when the glint of a knife appeared and she heard the man working on the lock.

She backed into the small break-room just as he opened the door. Her heart pounded when she caught her first clear view of the man. It was Anderson Coldhouse! She remained frozen, afraid to move lest he catch the movement.

He was going through the papers stacked on the counter. She glanced at the office door. She had to get that blood-stained envelope and get out before Coldhouse knew she was here.

She was about to slip back across the hallway when the bell at the front door chimed again.

"What the hell are you doing in here?" Coldhouse growled. "I thought I told you to stay in the car!"

"A call came over the line. Someone noticed you entering the building."

"Did you tell them you were in the area and would check it out?"

"Yeah."

"What exactly did you tell them, Bert?"

"I told them I was in the area on my way to pick up some lunch," Bert answered in an edgy tone.

"Did you mention I was with you?"

"Nah, Anderson, I didn't say nothing about you."

"That's good," Coldhouse replied.

"Why?" Bert asked.

SOMETHING ABOUT AIMEE

Aimee was wondering the same thing as she captured the entire exchange on her cell phone when she heard the familiar pop of gunfire. She jumped and lifted a hand to her mouth to smother her horrified gasp.

"You've become a liability, partner, and I don't do liabilities," Coldhouse said.

The plexiglass was a mess of cracks radiating from the bullet hole. Coldhouse walked around the counter, pushed open the door, and stepped back into the lobby. Through the open door, Aimee saw Bert lying on the ground and Anderson aiming the gun at his partner again. He pulled the trigger two more times. She jumped with each shot. The gun he was holding looked like the one Stanley kept in the box under the counter.

She eyed the door to the back office, then the hallway leading to the employee exit. If she went back into the office, she would be trapped.

Deciding her best chance of escaping was to do it now, she stepped out of the break-room and slid along the wall as quietly as she could. Her heart pounded, and she kept her eyes glued to the reception door. She was halfway to the exit when Coldhouse turned around and walked through the door. Their eyes connected, his wide with surprise, hers flashing with fear and hatred.

A cruel smile curved his lips as he slowly raised the gun. There was nowhere for her to hide. She gripped the cell phone. If she was going to die, she needed to hide it. It was the only evidence she had against him.

"Payback is a bitch, sweetheart," he said.

Aimee shook her head. "You won't get away with this," she forced past her frozen vocal cords.

Coldhouse chuckled. "Oh, I think I will. Especially when it becomes known that you killed a good cop today. He had a lovely wife, and a son and daughter, too."

"Why did you do this? Does it have anything to do with a blood-stained envelope?"

Anderson's eyes narrowed. "So, the envelope arrived." His eyes flickered to the open office door. "Thanks for your help," he said before he pulled the trigger.

Aimee flinched, but the gun clicked instead of firing. Anderson frowned and pulled the trigger again and again. The reprieve kicked Aimee into motion. She toppled the water cooler outside the office door and took off running.

She probably only had another few seconds until he gave up on Stanley's gun and remembered that he had his own gun holstered on his belt.

The wood on the door frame beside her exploded from the impact of a bullet. She pushed open the door and burst outside. Turning to the left, she ran as fast as she could down the alley, turning right at the end before crossing the next street.

She ignored Anderson's curses as he followed. The streets were her home, and she knew every place in this part of the city where she could slip through and disappear.

She ran as far as she could before her recovering lungs forced her to a fast walk. She looked back and didn't see him. She covered her mouth, trying to smother her coughs as she struggled to catch her breath.

She had to find a safe place to hide. Sirens filled the air, and Aimee slid down behind a dumpster as police vehicles flashed past on their way to Becker's. She knew what would have happened by now at the courier office. She had witnessed it enough times.

Leaning her head back against the wall, she closed her eyes as tears streamed down her cheeks. Coldhouse would find the file he was looking for and either hide or destroy it. Then, he would play the part of outraged partner and declare her a cop killer. The unspoken word among the Blues would be to kill on sight.

She lowered her head. Coldhouse had been wearing gloves, he had used Stanley's gun and shot his partner through the partition. He would probably lay out some evidence and call it either a robbery gone bad or drugs. It would probably be drugs.

He'll say I was running drugs for Biggy and using Stanley as a cover, she thought.

She fingered the phone in her hand. This was bigger than just Coldhouse. This was some serious international shit—and it involved Qadir. She swallowed down the bile that rose in her throat as she remembered the images of the people Coldhouse's brother had murdered.

She needed help. Help that was higher up the food chain than the local police.

Another cop car flew by, and Aimee knew it would be too dangerous to make it downtown during the daylight hours. She needed to hide until dark.

Twelve

Qadir frowned when he saw the police vehicles parked in front of the Harris building. He was about to step out of the limo when he saw Tarek exit the building and stride toward the car. A bodyguard pulled the door open and Tarek entered the limo with a sharp command in Arabic. In seconds, the limo pulled away from the curb.

"What happened?" Qadir demanded.

"Carthmen is dead."

"His heart?"

Tarek shook his head. "A bullet to the head. It looks like a suicide."

Qadir studied his brother's face. "You don't sound convinced."

Tarek shook his head again. "The angle was wrong—Carthmen was left handed. The gun was in his right hand."

Qadir lifted an eyebrow. "Murdered? By whom and why?"

Tarek gave him a grim smile. "I can't answer the who, but I can guess at the why. I've been doing some deeper research into Carthmen's business dealings, following the money. It led to a shell company owned by Atri Holdings. The name sounded familiar."

"Atri Holdings belongs to Andrius Bronislav, the Lithuanian billionaire," Qadir replied.

"Yes, and he's good friends with Rashid al Hamid."

Qadir grimaced in distaste.

Rashid's mother, Dima, was Qadir's great aunt. Rashid's father was Faiz al Hamid, a sheikh of the northern tribe who had ruled with a brutal sword thirty-two years ago. Faiz had tried to strip Jawahir of its wealth, killing thousands of people in the process. The marriage of Dima and Faiz was intended to heal the Civil War, but once Faiz had an heir, Dima mysteriously perished in a riding accident.

Rashid had all the ruthless callousness of his late father, but it was extremely unlikely that he would ever rule. His chances of rising to the throne of Jawahir had significantly lessened with the birth of Qadir and his brothers. Rashid's animosity flared when policies were put in place to diminish the already limited power he held in the cabinet.

"Do you think Rashid was behind the attack? What did Carthmen have to do with it?" Qadir asked.

"Carthmen could have been convenient. What I know is this: There is a connection between Carthmen and Rashid through Atri Holdings. Atri Holdings has been trying to sell our computer chips to countries on our banned list. Unrest is growing in our northern region. One of our mines collapsed, a transport of raw materials was bombed, and a man I have on the inside hasn't checked in for over a month. Do I believe Rashid was behind the attack on you and the killing of Carthmen? Yes. Can I prove it? No. Various pieces of evidence suggest that he's the one stirring the pot, but I think it is time I check out what is going on there in person."

"Make it happen," Qadir stated.

The limo slowed. Qadir frowned when he saw the street leading to Becker's closed off. A small crowd was gathering behind a row of cars.

A news reporter stood with her back to the building, talking as two people from the coroner's office emerged from the building with a body in a large black bag. Qadir could feel the blood drain from his face as he took in the scene. He reached for the door, but Tarek covered his hand and shook his head.

"Let Hasan find out what is happening," Tarek advised.

Qadir wanted to protest, but he knew his brother was right. The media was already becoming curious about their presence. He gave a terse nod. Tarek pulled out his cell phone and rapidly spoke to Hasan.

Qadir watched Hasan exit the vehicle in front of the limo and walk over to a police officer standing near the edge of the crowd. The man looked to be of Middle Eastern descent.

Qadir's eyes moved back to the vehicle where the body had been deposited. The body in the black bag was too large to be Aimee. It could be Stanley—or one of the other men who worked there.

Hasan walked to the limo door. Qadir lowered the window far enough that he could see Hasan but no one could see in. Hasan bent down and spoke rapidly in a low voice.

"There was a police detective attempting to apprehend a woman who broke into Becker's. The detective was killed. A second officer was in the area and witnessed the shooting. He said that the detective confronted her, the woman opened fire, and she escaped out the back," Hasan said.

"What?" Qadir hissed.

"What happened to the woman?" Tarek asked.

Hasan shook his head. "There is a warrant out for her arrest."

Qadir was about to reply when his cell phone vibrated. He glanced at it, his eyes widening when he recognized the number. He closed the window at the same time he answered the phone.

"I didn't do it," Aimee's shaking voice immediately said.

"I know you didn't. Are you alright? Where are you?"

He glanced at Tarek who nodded. Tarek would trace Aimee's number.

"Qadir, it was—"

The sound of gunfire blared through the phone. The line went dead. Qadir closed his eyes.

"Aimee."

Tarek was speaking rapidly to one of his security men. Qadir's hand shook as he tried to call Aimee back. She had never set up her voicemail. He clutched his cell phone and stared blindly out of the window.

"The signal came from the old warehouse we found her in before," Tarek announced. He turned and gave the driver the address.

"There was gunfire," Qadir said in a voice devoid of emotion.

Tarek returned his grim look. "Aimee is smart. She will survive."

Qadir nodded. He gazed out at the blur of passing buildings and calculated that it would take them ten minutes to get to the warehouse. A lot could happen in ten minutes.

They were almost to the warehouse when sirens behind them forced his driver to pull over. Dread filled him when he saw the plumes of black smoke rising from the buildings. Four fire trucks passed them, followed by several police cars.

"No!" he whispered, pushing open the door to the limo.

"Qadir," Tarek called behind him.

Qadir ignored his brother and began running down the sidewalk. He cut through a side street and emerged on the other side less than a block from the warehouse. The building was engulfed in flames. Tarek stopped beside him, followed by his bodyguards. Qadir stood frozen, staring at the flames and feeling as if he were trapped in a nightmare.

"Qadir," Tarek said, placing a hand on his shoulder.

He shrugged off his brother's hand and walked slowly down the sidewalk. The shouts of firemen and the loud sounds from their equipment drifted across the water. A tugboat with a water cannon was attacking the blaze from the harbor side.

"Qadir, there is nothing we can do here. The media will arrive soon. Go. I will find out what has happened and report back to you," Tarek encouraged.

"Find her, Tarek. Find her and bring her back to me," he softly ordered, his gaze locked on the building as the roof caved in and flames reached greedily for the sky.

Dawn was breaking over the horizon when Tarek finally returned. Qadir looked at his brother's drawn, tired face. Tarek shoved his hands into his pockets and stared at him, visibly struggling to find the right words.

"Tell me," he ordered.

"The body of a young woman was found. The body—" Tarek took a deep breath. "The body was burned beyond recognition. I will receive a copy of the coroner's report once it is finished," he said, looking away.

"What are you not telling me?" he demanded.

Tarek looked back at him, his eyes filled with grief. "I overheard a firefighter mention that the woman had been shot," he confessed.

Pain seared through Qadir like a hot knife. He took a step back as it hit him. The shield he had been building over the past few hours to protect his heart burst under an intense wave of grief. He shook his head when Tarek lifted a comforting hand toward him.

"Find out… find out what happened. I want to know everything, Tarek —and I want to destroy whoever is behind this."

"I will make sure that it happens," Tarek vowed.

SOMETHING ABOUT AIMEE

Qadir turned away. The elevator door closed behind his brother, and his resolute facade cracked. Alone again, he stared with unseeing eyes at the sun rising over the city.

An uncontrollable trembling consumed his body and a harsh sound, like that of a wounded animal, broke the silence. Gasping for breath, Qadir sat down on the edge of the chair and did something he hadn't done since he was a very small boy. He cried.

Two weeks later, Qadir left New York for Jawahir. He had lost weight —and a piece of his soul. He held two reports in his hand. The first was the autopsy report from the coroner's office. He had memorized every detail, searching for some hope that there had been a mistake.

Young Caucasian female; age 20-24; five foot four inches tall; evidence of recent lung infection. Cause of death: 9mm bullet to the back of the head. Body burned over 100 percent.

The second report was from their informant in Rashid's inner circle— in a roundabout way. The informant had disappeared over a month ago and had finally been found—in pieces, but the FBI had gotten ahold of the informant's last desperate message and passed it on to Qadir.

It gave Qadir a target. It gave him the names of the individuals behind atrocities committed against his people—and he knew it was the reason for Aimee's death. She had given her life to save him and protect his people.

Tarek suspected that their spy had sent the photos via courier services in the hope of it making it through all the attempts to keep it quiet. Aimee would have discovered it when she was sorting the deliveries.

Colin Coldhouse must have tracked the document to Becker's Courier Service.

Colin was in charge of Andrius Bronislav's private security forces. In one of the photos in this report, he was the man standing over a line of dead nomads in Shedad, a mountainous region known for its rugged terrain.

Colin had a brother—Detective Anderson Coldhouse. Anderson was the detective who claimed to have witnessed Aimee shooting his partner, Bert Crank.

The brothers had been in special ops together before Anderson joined the NYPD five years ago and Colin started working for Bronislav in the Middle East and Asia. Anderson had only been in the Upper Manhattan office of the NYPD for six months. Colin had placed him there to find and kill the spy, then find the damning evidence and remove it, along with any witnesses, which included Carthmen. The informant in Rashid's inner circle had sent him the photos, too.

The attempt on Qadir's life using a couple of locals was mostly a distraction while Anderson hunted for the leaked evidence of their crimes, but it still had the possibility of succeeding and destabilizing the royal family more than all their efforts so far.

Anderson had left New York the night his partner died, claiming that he needed time to mourn. He boarded a private jet registered to a shell company of Atri Holdings and traveled to Lithuania.

Qadir looked up when Tarek entered the jet's cabin and sat in the seat opposite him. A steward appeared, and Tarek ordered a drink. Tarek's gaze flickered to the reports open in front of Qadir. They didn't speak until after the steward handed Tarek his glass and left the room.

"Father has ordered Rashid's arrest," Tarek said.

Qadir clenched his jaw. "What about Colin and Anderson Coldhouse? I want their heads on a platter," he coolly replied.

"Colin has disappeared and Anderson is hiding in one of Bronislav's mansions," Tarek answered.

"I want them both, Tarek. I don't care what it takes; make it happen," Qadir replied in a hard voice.

"Oh, I will, brother. I will," Tarek promised.

Thirteen

ATLANTA, GEORGIA
THREE YEARS LATER

"And cut! That's a wrap. Great job, everyone!" the director called.

Aimee held out her hand to help the guy she had just knocked down stand up. Lou grasped it and stiffly rose to his feet. He rubbed his stomach gingerly.

She shook her head. "I didn't even make contact."

"It's the thought, A. You make it look so real. You know, we could do some practicing over dinner tonight," he teased.

With a smile and a shake of her head, Aimee rolled her eyes and walked away. She looked around the set of the action thriller currently under production. This had been her last scene. If the executives reviewed the film and it was a take, she would be heading back to Los Angeles tomorrow night.

"Hi, Aimee," Habib called.

Aimee waved at the man who was slightly younger than herself. He was working here while he went to film school. She genuinely liked Habib. Sure, she felt a little guilty about her reasons for talking to him sometimes, but she would grasp at any glimpse of the life that had been stolen from her. They walked side by side.

"Hi, Habib. How are things going back home?"

He laughed. "The same as they were yesterday," he teased.

"Well, that's good," she replied.

They headed for the large catering tent. She grabbed a bottle of water out of a large ice-filled bin. Habib grabbed a tray full of sandwiches, a bag of potato chips, and a soda and they walked to a table.

She sat down on a plastic chair, listening to him as he told her about his parents and siblings back in Jawahir. Aimee soaked up every word, her heart aching with love and longing for Qadir.

"So, Sadi told me last night that there is to be a royal wedding!" Habib said with excitement.

Aimee stiffened and stared at him. "A royal wedding? Wh-who is getting married?"

Habib grinned at her. "Sheikh Qadir."

"Qadir is getting married?" she repeated.

"Yes! At least that is what Basma told me last night when we chatted," Habib said.

Aimee listened in silence as Habib talked about how the King had decided it was time for Qadir to marry and arranged it with a mystery bride. The press was going crazy trying to find out who she was, which was exactly why the King was protecting her identity.

Aimee nodded at the right times and murmured barely audible responses as Habib continued regaling her with speculation about the mysterious princess betrothed to the future King of Jawahir. All she wanted to do was find a place to hide and cry. She'd known this day would come, but she still wasn't ready for it.

She suddenly pushed her chair back and stood up. He stopped mid-sentence and stared up at her with a startled expression. She gave him a strained, crooked smile.

"I forgot I needed to check in with Merv. You know how he gets if you forget," she lied, turning away from him.

"Yeah… well, maybe we can get together later," Habib called behind her.

"Yeah, see you later," she replied.

Aimee walked over to the stunt double training tent. She didn't feel like working out, but she did it anyway because it was a great way to get people to leave her alone. It also gave her time to think—which could be a good thing but wasn't at the moment.

The incident three years ago in New York had changed her life forever. Her carefree days of living where she wanted, visiting friends, working for Stanley, and loving Qadir had ended overnight. Now, she had a new last name and a new career.

Grief and regret filled her. The depressing knowledge that she had no one to blame but herself for losing Qadir weighed on her conscience. Over the last three years, she had done a lot of self-reflection and realized that things could have been different if she had made different choices—like going to Qadir instead of the FBI. Even now, she fought with the realization that she had done exactly what Yolanda had taught her to do—run and hide when things get tough.

Her fears of commitment and her reluctance to trust had overshadowed everything. For quite a while she had camouflaged her fear in a self-righteous assertion that she was protecting Qadir, but in reality, she was only trying to protect her own fragile heart.

She closed her eyes against the tears welling up and fought against the memories of what transpired after she had slipped into the old warehouse. It was impossible. She still had nightmares of that day and how she barely escaped—and the terrible decisions she had made that left her lonely, aching, and yet still too afraid to reach out to Qadir and correct her mistakes.

∼

Three Years Ago

The cold air burned her lungs, and she fought against another fit of coughing. She reached into the pocket of her long coat and pulled out the inhaler Dr. Fuah had given her. Popping the top, she inhaled two puffs. The relief was almost immediate.

She pocketed the inhaler and slipped through the opening in the gate. She darted across the open parking lot before disappearing around the side. In less than a minute, she had entered through the window.

Tears burned her eyes as she thought of Qadir. She had to let him know what was happening—not only here but back in his home country. All those people murdered—the children—there had to be something he could do to stop it.

She crossed the warehouse, heading for the office and the box she had hidden upstairs. She would wait until darkness fell before making her way downtown to the Federal building. The FBI would surely know what to do and they were less likely to have a connection with the local police—at least, with Coldhouse—with *either* of the Coldhouses.

Aimee climbed the stairs to the office and pushed open the door. She had only taken a couple of steps inside when she felt a knife pressed against her back. She froze, her breath forming a cloud of fog as she waited.

"G-give me your coat," a soft, feminine voice demanded.

Aimee held her hands up and nodded. "You staying here? It's not so bad," she said.

"How-how w-would you know?" the young woman asked.

"I've lived here for the past six months. I'm Aimee. What's your name?" she asked.

There was a short pause before the woman answered, "Kylie."

"Hi, Kylie. I'm going to put my hands down and take off my coat," Aimee said.

"Don't try nothin'," Kylie choked out.

Aimee could hear Kylie trying to suppress a cough. "I won't. There's an inhaler in my right pocket. The doc gave it to me. Sounds like you could use it. I've got some antibiotics in there, too, for my lungs. As long as you aren't allergic to them, you might want to take them. There aren't many left, but it might help," she suggested.

She felt the pressure of the knife disappear and breathed a sigh of relief. If sacrificing her coat and medicine helped her get out of here, she would gladly do it. She removed her outer coat, thankful she wore several layers of clothing under one of Qadir's thick cashmere sweaters. Turning, she held out the coat to Kylie who took it with a moan of pleasure.

Aimee stepped forward and helped button the coat. Kylie's hands were shaking so badly that she was having trouble. The girl warily watched her as Aimee retrieved a glove from each pocket.

"Why are you helping me?" Kylie asked as she allowed Aimee to put the gloves on her.

Aimee looked up and gave Kylie a strained smile. "Because we aren't so different," she said.

Kylie looked around the room. "This your spot?" she asked.

Aimee shrugged. "It was."

Kylie looked at her. "I got another spot that's better. I was scoping this place out, but it's too cold. I'm keeping the coat—and the other stuff. You got any money?" she demanded, waving the knife in her hand.

The smile on Aimee's face faded. "No. You've got everything I own in that coat," she lied.

Kylie nodded and began backing toward the door. "That's the way of the street," she replied, backing out of the door.

Aimee stood in the freezing room, shivering, and listened as Kylie descended the steps. She didn't bother going after the girl. Aimee had enough troubles. She really didn't need to fight a desperate girl with a knife. At least Kylie didn't ask for Aimee's knit cap.

Turning away, Aimee crossed the room and pulled open an old exhaust vent. She reached inside and drew out a shoebox containing a dozen pictures of herself and Yolanda and the few precious things Yolanda had found when she discovered Aimee in the alley. Next, she grabbed a plastic bag containing a pile of emergency clothing. It included another heavy coat. The coat was worn, but it was clean and it would keep her from freezing.

She rose back to her feet, slipped on the coat, and buttoned it up. Breathing on the tips of her fingers to warm them, she pulled her cell phone out of her back pocket and dialed Qadir's number. She held her breath when the phone rang. He answered it on the second ring.

"I didn't do it," she said the moment she heard his voice.

"I know you didn't. Are you alright? Where are you?" Qadir demanded.

A quiver of relief flooded her. He would believe her. She had to warn him. "Qadir, it was—"

The sound of gunfire caused her to jump and her thumb hit the disconnect button. Crouching, she peered out of the door.

Anderson Coldhouse stood over Kylie's inert body. He fired another shot into the back of Kylie's head.

Aimee pressed her fist against her mouth. Tears for the other woman burned her eyes. She had done this. She should have known that Coldhouse would follow her.

He cursed and looked around. She quickly twisted away from the door and leaned up against the wall, her heart pounding. He must have realized he had killed the wrong person.

Metal hit concrete, and the first whiff of crude oil and burning flesh hit her. Nausea threatened to overcome her. She covered her nose and mouth with her arm, afraid that she would start coughing and alert Coldhouse that she was there.

Black smoke quickly filled the warehouse. Aimee knew she had to get out immediately. The building was old and still had most of the original wooden structure. It wouldn't take long for it to go up like a torch. That was one reason why she made sure there was an alternative exit before staying here.

She crawled across the floor of the office, dragged her bed from the wall, shoved aside the cardboard she used as insulation, and worked the piece of metal sheeting out of the way. The hole beneath was revealed.

Smoke billowed into the room and her cough caused pain in her throat and lungs.

Stuffing the contents of the shoebox into her pockets and her cell phone into her bra, she wiggled through the hole. She grabbed the drain pipe and pulled herself the rest of the way through, sliding down the pipe until her feet hit the first bracket.

Heat radiated from the exterior walls and flames licked through the cracks.

She slid down the pipe the rest of the way to the ground, stumbling back when a loud explosion rocked the building. She almost fell but caught herself.

Near the staircase, there were several old barrels full of some kind of solvent left over from whatever manufacturing had been done in the building before. They were exploding now.

Sirens blared in the distance. Aimee turned and ran between the building and the water. Coldhouse was still close.

Tears streamed down her cheeks as she desperately sought a place of refuge. She pulled her cell phone out of her pocket. The battery light flashed. It was dead.

Several blocks away, she crouched in an alley behind a dumpster. She sank down to the ground and drew her knees up, wrapping her arms around them.

Engulfed in numbness, Aimee sat in the alley until darkness descended. She was cold and stiff by the time she felt it was safe to move. Keeping her head down, she stayed off the main streets and in the shadows as much as possible. It took her over an hour to get downtown to the Federal Building.

She stood outside—watching—terrified of what would happen if she didn't go inside and terrified of what would happen if she did. It was nearly midnight by the time she forced her legs to carry her across the street. She pulled open the door and stepped inside the confined space between the second set of doors. The security guard near the metal detectors rose to his feet at the sight of her.

Aimee was suddenly self-conscious of the fact that her face was dirty and her clothing probably still smelled of smoke. Stiffening her shoulders, she pulled open the second door and entered the FBI building.

"Can I help you?" the security guard inquired.

Tears suddenly blurred Aimee's eyes and she silently nodded. It took several seconds before she gained enough composure to speak. When she did, her voice trembled with exhaustion and fear.

"I-I need to speak to someone about-about a series of murders," she finally said.

The guard frowned. "You should call the NYPD for that."

She gave him a look of utter hopelessness. "It was a police officer who did the killings—and he is trying to kill me to keep me from telling anyone about that—and other horrible things. I don't have anywhere else to turn. I need someone more powerful who can keep me safe."

The guard's expression softened. "If you have anything in your pockets, empty them out and walk through."

Aimee nodded, placed the dead cell phone in the gray plastic bin, and walked through the metal detector. The guard nodded to another man behind a long desk. She gave him a wobbly smile, retrieved her phone, and walked over.

"I would like to report the murders of several people both here and in a country called Jawahir that were committed by a man named Anderson Coldhouse and his brother, Colin Coldhouse," she said in a quiet voice.

The man studied her tired face before he picked up the phone and called someone else. Within minutes, a man and a woman stepped out of the elevator to her right. The woman offered her hand.

"I'm Agent Angela Hartley. This is Davis. You have information pertaining to Colin Coldhouse?" Agent Hartley inquired.

"Yes, and the murders his brother committed this afternoon," she said. She held up her dead cell phone.

"Please follow me," Agent Hartley said.

~

PRESENT DAY

Aimee was distracted from her memories when several cast members entered the exercise area. She hadn't even realized that she was lying on the floor with her eyes closed until then. The group called out a good-natured hello to her before they split up and climbed on different machines. Aimee rose to her feet and quietly left the tent.

She had shared everything that night with Agent Hartley and Davis. Hartley had found a charger for her phone and Aimee showed them the photos she had taken of the photographs along with the video of

Anderson Coldhouse killing his partner, Bert. It had been difficult sharing what happened at the warehouse.

Hartley had taken her cell phone. Dawn was breaking over the horizon when she was led to the parking garage. Hartley explained that Aimee would need to be kept under close guard until Anderson Coldhouse was caught.

Aimee had begged Hartley to let her call Qadir, but Hartley said it was too dangerous. Anderson—and his brother, Colin—had ways of tracking the phone call. Hartley assured her that Qadir would be notified that Aimee was in their custody and safe.

It took Aimee over six months to discover that Agent Hartley had lied. Why the FBI wanted Qadir to believe she had been killed in the fire at the warehouse was still a mystery to her. Every time she pressed the new agent in charge of her case about it, they gave her some vague lecture about international protocol and the sensitive nature of the case.

The first six months had been a blur. She had been transferred from one safe house to another after two attempts on her life. How Bronislav or the Coldhouse brothers even knew she was still alive was a mystery since Anderson would have believed she was trapped in the warehouse when he set it on fire.

In the end, her death was faked again, and she was placed in the witness protection program. She was given a new identity with all the correct paperwork—something she'd never had before—a new career, an apartment, and she was told that she must contact no one from her past.

Hartley had stressed that even if the Coldhouse brothers were eventually captured, there was no way the government could do anything about Andrius Bronislav, a foreign national. Her life and anyone she knew would always be in danger.

After one agent was killed and another was seriously wounded protecting her, she believed them. Her heart hurt every day for Qadir, and she hungrily searched for any news about him.

When she met Habib working on a set two years ago and found out he was from Jawahir and his older sister worked in the palace, she had befriended him. Their friendship really had grown beyond her using him for information about Qadir. She cared about him.

Now she almost wished she had cut off everything from her old life. Knowing Qadir was getting married hurt, even though she knew she should be happy for him. After all, he had no idea that she was alive.

Aimee collected her belongings from the set trailer. After placing her skateboard on the ground, she adjusted her backpack, and took off for the hotel rented by the studio for the cast and crew. Depression was bringing her down hard, and she wondered if death might have been a kinder fate.

I can get through this, she told herself.

She kept telling herself that over and over as her wheels clicked on the lines of the sidewalk.

Fourteen

Andrius Bronislav sat aboard the sleek private jet reading the current report that Colin Coldhouse had prepared for him. Colin's company, Cold Methods Security, lived up to its name.

Colin had recently cleared a troubled area in Belarus and paved the way for a new manufacturing site. The new microchip factory would cost him billions, but it would eventually allow him to flood the market with chips designed with a specific flaw that would allow his company backdoor access to proprietary data around the world. Such information could be sold to the right people for trillions.

The issue he faced now was that he still needed the resources found in Jawahir. Whoever controlled that small country controlled the future of technology.

The only way forward was to overthrow the current ruling family or kill them off. Once they were gone, Rashid would be released from prison and succeed to the position of ruler—under Andrius's control. First though, Andrius needed access to those trade secrets Jawahir was protecting. It wasn't all about the minerals and gem stones in that country, though those were important. There was information to be had, information vital to manufacturing his own microchips.

His cell phone vibrated. Andrius connected and lifted it to his ear as he continued to thumb through the report on the compact serving tray in front of him.

"Excellent job in Belarus," he said as a greeting.

"I always aim to please. Thank you for the generous payment," Colin stated.

"I have another job for you," Andrius replied, pausing on one image.

"I'm ready," Colin answered.

"Qadir Saif-Ad-Din. I need specific information before he is terminated," he said.

There was silence on the other end. Andrius knew that Colin was remembering how he had barely escaped Jawahir with his life. The man had the scars to prove it.

"This won't be easy," Colin replied. "He goes nowhere without his security team."

Andrius's eyebrow lifted. "Are you saying you can't do the job?" he inquired.

"I said it wouldn't be easy. This will cost you double the normal rate," Colin answered in a terse tone.

Andrius smiled. "Agreed. I need him alive long enough to give me the information I require. I will send you what I need. I don't care how you get it; just make sure you do, or there will be no payment. Terminate him when you have it. The rest of the Saif-Ad-Din family will follow."

"Finally. Do you have a timeline?" Colin asked.

"On second thought, I want you to break Rashid out of prison first. Then, take care of Qadir. If things go south, we can always lay the blame at Rashid's feet."

"Yes, sir."

"Qadir, wait up," Tarek called from the end of the hallway.

Qadir ground his teeth together. He was not in the mood to deal with any more family members. The meeting with his father had not gone well, and he needed time to calm down.

"What is it, Tarek?" he growled.

Tarek's eyes were wary, and the crooked lift at the corner of his mouth told Qadir that his brother would avoid confrontation and try cajoling. Qadir rolled his shoulders and sighed deeply.

"I guess your conversation with father didn't go any better than the first one," Tarek commented.

Qadir shook his head. "No, if anything, it was worse. I'm thirty-three. I won't have anyone, including our father, tell me who and when I'm to marry."

"Did he reveal the unfortunate woman's name?"

"No, which makes it even worse. He refuses, saying he knows exactly what I will do when I find out. He says he will reveal who he has chosen at the right moment and not until then. In the meantime, every press office and entertainment rag in the world is speculating about this."

Tarek's face twisted into a grimace of distaste. "I have to admit that I'm glad Father is focused on you. You know how he can be when he makes a decision."

Qadir shot his brother a dark look. "I will be leaving this afternoon. I want to meet with the northern tribe leaders and review how the infrastructure is progressing. The new bridge over the Yakin River should be complete," he said.

Tarek nodded. "I've cleared my schedule. I want to go with you."

Qadir frowned. "Is there a problem?"

Tarek shook his head. "Rumors that I wish to check out."

"You know we have personnel for that," Qadir dryly replied.

Tarek laughed. "Yes, I know. This is a matter I would prefer to handle myself. Besides, going out into the field helps keep me sharp."

Qadir chuckled and shook his head. "You are doing it to get away from the palace before Father finds a bride for you."

Tarek grinned. "There are worse reasons to run away."

ATLANTA, GEORGIA

Aimee was in the middle of packing her backpack for her early morning flight back to L.A. when a knock on the door snapped her back from her gloomy thoughts. She glanced at the clock. It was almost eight in the evening. There was only one person who would be knocking—Habib.

She crossed the room and peered through the peek-hole. Habib was shifting from side to side like he had ants in his pants. She opened the door when she saw him raise his hand to knock again. Surprise gripped her when he impatiently pushed past her into the room. Habib was always polite and always nervous whenever she invited him into her room without having others there.

"What's got you all riled up?" she demanded, shutting the door and facing him.

He was pacing back and forth in front of the window. He stopped and looked at her with a troubled expression. Concerned, she lifted her hand toward him and stepped closer.

"What happened, Habib? Did something happen to one of your sisters or brothers? Are your parents alright?"

He waved his hand in the air. "They are fine. They are all fine. It isn't them. It's the royal family!" he said.

"What do you mean?"

"Two of the royal sons, Sheikh Qadir and Sheikh Tarek were targeted by terrorists as they were traveling north!" Habib rubbed his hands together in agitation.

Aimee grabbed his arms, propelled him to the edge of her bed, and made him sit down. She cupped his cheeks between her palms, and his eyes locked with hers.

"I want you to take a deep breath, and tell me exactly what happened," she said.

He nodded and took several deep breaths. She pulled the rolling chair from her desk and sat down in front of him. He started to rise, but she held his hands to keep him still. He sank back on the bed and stared at her.

"The Jawahir people love our royal family. They have done so much for all of us. I would never have been able to come here and take the classes in a field I love if not for the scholarships they award each person," he began.

"I know. You've told me this before. What I want to know is what happened to Qadir and Tarek," she said.

Habib took another deep, calming breath and nodded. "I told you that my older sister, Rahat, works in the palace. She is a junior secretary to Queen Ihab. She swore me to secrecy. The news isn't out to the media yet. She said Sheikh Qadir's transports were attacked as they crossed the Aljibal Alsawda'."

"Who attacked? Are they okay?"

Habib lifted his shoulders. "Tarek was gravely wounded. Nearly a dozen men were killed. Qadir was dragged out of the vehicle and taken. Rahat said—" He bit his lip and looked at her with worried eyes. "Rahat said the initial reports describe the men as foreigners. The leader sounded American."

Ice swept through her veins and sent a chill down her spine. Aimee sat back in the chair and rubbed her arms. The photos she had given the FBI three years ago flashed through her mind. An American was behind those atrocities. An American who was still at large.

"Can you show me where the attack occurred?" she asked in a trembling voice.

"Yes," Habib said, pulling out his cell phone.

Aimee switched from the chair to the bed so she could see the map.

"The Aljibal Alsawda', or the Black Mountains, are near the northern border. The territory is extremely harsh and rugged. It is well known for its extensive cave systems. "

Over the last three years she had read anything and everything she could about the country. Habib pointed to the region where the attack took place. There were hundreds of paths feathering out from the main road leading through the mountains. It would take months to find where the attackers went—if the Jawahir royal army ever did.

A niggling thought began bugging her. She took Habib's phone and studied the map. She had seen a map very similar to this one—only with more detail.

Like a bubble bursting, she remembered the bloody envelope she found in Stanley's office three years ago. The map inside had circles on it showing places where a hidden base might be.

"Habib, do you have any relatives in your country that might be interested in driving me somewhere? It... might be dangerous for them."

Habib frowned. "You are going to my country?"

She looked at him with a shaky smile. "Yes. You see, I might know where this American took Qadir, but I'm going to need your help."

Fifteen

ALJIBAL ALSAWDA'
(BLACK MOUNTAINS OF JAWAHIR)

Colin cursed under his breath. His brother had screwed up the mission by not securing the area. He should have known better than to trust Anderson.

The unmistakable sound of military helicopters searching the area had forced him and his team to seek cover in the caves along the road. Anderson's team was cut off twenty kilometers to the north.

They would have made it across the border to safety if someone had not seen and reported the attack on the royal convoy. He didn't know who had, but he looked forward to finding out. He had lost five good men to a sniper. They had gone down like cans on a fence before his people could take cover.

Regardless, Sheikh Qadir Saif-Ad-Din was in one of Anderson's vehicles, and Tarek Saif-Ad-Din was among the dead. Those were good things.

Now, it was up to him to get them all out of this mess. Cut off from using the main road by the Jawahir Royal Military, Colin accepted that they would not make it to the base tonight.

After she swore Habib to secrecy, Aimee shared her past with him. At first, she was hesitant to share much, but once she opened up, it was like a dam had burst, and she poured out most of what had happened to her.

Habib was shocked. Slowly, the shock turned to awe, then to determination. He said she might be the Nasira of Jawahir—the Defender. In the ancient story, the Nasira was a woman who would someday cross the world to save Jawahir for the sake of her long lost love.

By morning, Aimee had booked her plane ticket from L.A. to Jawahir, and it was agreed that Abdal would take her anywhere she wished to go. According to Habib, Abdal was fearless, knew the country better than anyone, and loved the royal family almost as much as he did.

Aimee landed at LAX with just enough time to make it to her apartment, shower, change, and grab the map before she took a share-ride back to the airport.

Twenty-nine hours later, she stepped off the plane in Jawahir and passed through customs with just her passport, some money, and her backpack. Habib had promised that anything she needed, Abdal could supply for her.

Aimee scanned the group holding up signs. One of the men held up a sign that said 'Habib's Cousin.'

"Abdal?" Aimee inquired.

"*Tahiaatun*, Nasira of Jawahir," Abdal greeted.

"*Tahiaatun*. I'm Aimee," she said, holding out her hand.

Abdal grasped her hand and bowed over it with a beaming smile. Aimee released a tired laugh. Abdal was in his late twenties, and he had an infectious smile. His irises were a deep dark brown, and his eyes sparkled with his vivacious spirit.

"Hello, Aimee. Come with me. I will be your willing servant," he said.

Aimee fell into step beside Abdal. She was wearing jeans, an oversized T-shirt, a light jean jacket, and a pair of well-worn dark brown ankle boots. In contrast, Abdal was wearing the clothing typical of the region: a long, white tunic called a *dishdasha* with short sherwal trousers and a white headscarf.

"Did you get the list of what I need from Habib?" she asked as she followed him outside.

"Yes, I have everything. I have to admit I am very curious about some of the items," he said with a smile.

A young woman stood next to the old Toyota Camry they were walking toward. She was dressed in a wide, long abayas and a dark blue hijab that showed strands of her black hair.

Aimee stopped in her tracks. "Who is she?"

Abdal looked back and forth between them, frowning as he motioned for her to continue to the car.

Aimee shook her head. "*Man hi almar'a?* Who is the woman?" she repeated.

"This is my sister, Selima. She will travel with us. It is not proper for me to travel alone with you."

Aimee felt her stomach clench. "No, she mustn't come with us," she said in a low voice.

"Selima is very good. You will not know she is there," he promised, motioning again for her to get in the car.

Aimee shook her head. "Abdal, I need you—only you—to drive me to the places I need to go. It will be dangerous. I don't want to endanger Selima."

Abdal smiled. "Selima will be good. Trust me, Aimee Nasira of Jawahir. Many of the women of Jawahir are warriors. They have fought beside our men for centuries."

Selima opened the back door of the car for her. The windows in the back were tinted a darker color than the front. Aimee mentally cursed and climbed into the car. Selima sat in the front seat while Abdal hurried around to the driver's side and climbed in.

"Welcome to Jawahir," Selima said with a warm smile.

Aimee bowed her head in greeting. "How much did Habib tell you about my trip here?"

"Very little," Abdal said. "He felt it would be better not to write things out. The items he asked for are common and could have easily been for him. I do not understand why you needed a man's outfit and a worn ball, but I have all the items Habib requested."

Aimee pulled the map out of her jacket's inside pocket and sat forward. She pointed and said, "I need to go to these three places."

Selima frowned. "These are near where the attack on Sheikh Qadir and Tarek took place."

"Yes," Aimee replied.

Abdal glanced over his shoulder at her before returning his attention to the traffic. "The Royal Military is searching the area," he warned.

"I expect it is," she said.

"Not quite. These are west of where the JRM is currently searching. May we ask why you wish to go there?" Selima inquired.

"Because I think one of those spots is where Qadir was taken."

"How do you know about these places?" Abdal asked.

"I found the map three years ago… along with some other photographs."

"Why didn't you notify the JRM about this?" Abdal asked, glancing at her in the rear view mirror.

"And tell them what? That I'm an American who found a map in a bloody envelope three years ago and I think I know where their Crown Prince is being held? They would either laugh me out of the country or lock me up."

Aimee blew out a slow breath, sat back, and looked out of the window. She didn't add that she was lousy at working with others and still had major trust issues. The only reason she was sitting in the car with Abdal was because of her friendship with Habib.

There were many pedestrians looking at the fashionable shops lining the street. The cafés were packed. The city reflected the wealth of the nation. High tech mixed with centuries-old architecture.

"There was a photograph of an American man," Aimee continued. "He did some terrible things here. I think he's the one who has Qadir, and I think these markings indicate his bases in the region."

"This American—do you know his name?" Abdal asked.

"Yes." She paused. "I don't actually know *for sure* that he is behind it," she hedged.

Selima watched her carefully as she said, "Our sources say Colin Coldhouse was hired by Andrius Bronislav to capture Sheikh Saif-Ad-Din."

Aimee stiffened at the mention of Coldhouse.

Selima continued, "We did not receive the information until after the attack. Whoever reported it saved the life of Sheikh Tarek. Unfortunately, eight highly skilled members of the Royal Guard were killed."

Suspicion flared inside Aimee. She hadn't shared everything with Habib, but she had trusted him when he said he knew someone who could help her. Now her old insecurities rose up, and she wondered if she had made a mistake.

"Who are you?" she demanded.

"I am Selima Abd Wahhab, of the RIS, the Royal Intelligence Service."

"I'm Abdal, Habib's cousin, and also a member of the RIS, though I am usually behind a keyboard and not out in the field like Selima."

Aimee looked out the window in silence, ignoring Selima's intense stare. It wasn't often that she was wrong about someone. Habib had lied.

"We owe you a great debt, Ms. Jones," Selima said. "The information you gave to your government three years ago was passed on to us and saved many lives. Habib told us what you gave up to do this. Let me assure you that the royal family, the JRM, and our people recognize you as our Nasira of Jawahir."

Aimee's face flushed with guilt. She hadn't given up anything—she had thrown everything away. If she could save Qadir now, it was the least she could do for him. She had learned her lesson and wouldn't make the same mistake again.

"The victims of Bronislav's atrocities will be avenged," Selima said. "The sanctions placed upon him have had a rippling effect. He is a desperate man."

"Desperate men are dangerous—and he has Qadir," she said.

Sixteen

Qadir stumbled on a loose rock but kept his balance. It wasn't easy considering his hands were bound behind his back. His head throbbed from dehydration and the blow to his temple he had received earlier. His ribs and a dozen other places hurt.

He gritted his teeth against the pain and scanned the darkness beyond. The drone of helicopters and aircraft had faded as darkness fell, and he knew that the search wouldn't resume until dawn.

His thoughts went back to the attack earlier in the day. It began when their attackers shot a mine buried in the road and it exploded in front of his lead escort vehicle.

Qadir was grateful for the spectacle—it was the whole reason his Search and Rescue teams had galvanized so quickly—but he was also full of anguish. How many of his guards had died? How many were wounded? He hoped Tarek, at least, had survived somehow.

The lead vehicle had veered off the narrow road to avoid the explosion. Fortunately, a large boulder had prevented it from going over the edge and down the mountain side. Men in a Hummer had slid to a halt in front of them and opened fire on the crashed SUV. The driver and two guards had been killed.

Then their attackers fired at Qadir's car, killing his driver. Two men in the SUVs behind them had been killed, and Tarek, who had been riding with Qadir, left the car, firing at the vehicles that had come up behind them as he raced over to one of the guards lying on the ground. The last Qadir had seen of Tarek was his bloody form falling over the road's edge and down the mountainside.

It was not a confirmed kill. Missing in action, maybe, but not dead, Qadir told himself.

After the frontal and rear attacks, there had been another attack on the left, less steep side of the road. Qadir had fired several rounds from his position in the vehicle before a tear gas grenade forced him to dive out.

While he had lain there dazed, he was surrounded and then dragged away. Qadir was deposited in the backseat of a Hummer, and they swiftly retreated.

A black bag was forced over his head, and he was thrust forward in the seat as his hands were bound behind his back. Once he was secured, a rough hand pushed him back against the seat and the butt of a rifle struck his temple.

Everything went black then.

When he awoke he was lying on his side on a hard, sandy floor. The sounds he heard indicated that they were in a cave. The bag was still over his head.

He took shallow breaths. There were a variety of accents in the voices around him.

"Mr. Coldhouse," a man had said.

Qadir had stiffened at the name.

"The Commander requests that we move out after dark."

Qadir had listened, unmoving with his eyes closed, as the man explained that they must abandon the vehicles because the main road would be secured by the JRM, the Jawahir Royal Military. Reconnaissance could be done at night, but it would only be effective if a vehicle was traveling with its lights on. The terrain was deadly enough during the day, there was no way to navigate it safely at night, not even with night vision goggles. If they wanted to avoid the main road, the only way to traverse the area was by camel, horseback, or foot.

Nearly an hour had passed before the cover over his head was removed, and he found himself staring into a pair of cold dark brown eyes. He remembered the man as the detective from New York who had tried to frame Aimee and then killed her.

Qadir had lunged at the man, striking him in the nose with his forehead. Anderson Coldhouse fell backward with a loud string of curses. Then Anderson strode forward and kicked him in the chest, knocking his breath from his lungs.

He had struggled to sit back up, his eyes glued to Coldhouse as the man wiped blood from his nose. Qadir had flexed his numb fingers, desperately wanting to wrap them around the man's throat. He would kill the bastard if it was the last thing he did.

"I see you remember me," Anderson had replied.

Qadir had bared his teeth. "Untie me, and I'll show you what I remember."

Anderson had wiped at his nose again and looked at the blood on his hand. "Sorry, your Highness, you'll have to live with the disappointment of not calling the shots here. You'll end up dead just like the bitch from New York, only I might not put a bullet in the back of your head before I set you on fire."

Qadir had lunged for Anderson again. A blow to his ribs knocked him back to the ground.

Anderson had squatted next to him and chuckled. "You know, I promised my brother I wouldn't kill you. I never promised him that I wouldn't make you wish I had."

∼

"Tell me again why we are on these filthy beasts?" Abdal complained.

"Horses are not filthy. Camels are filthy," Selima stated.

"It is the best way to get through the mountain passes," Aimee added.

Abdal shifted in the saddle. "I'm going to be sore for a week," he grumbled, unimpressed with their logic.

Selima shook her head and looked at Aimee. "This is why you do not pull a nerd into the field," she teased.

"I'm not a nerd, I'm a geek, and I have very specialized skills. I'd like to see you bring down half of Eastern Europe with one mouse click," Abdal retorted.

Aimee pretended to lick her finger and held it in the air with a sizzling sound. Selima chuckled while Abdal muttered about geeks being highly under-appreciated. They fell into a comfortable silence as they continued along the well-traveled, narrow trail.

Aimee felt a little guilty, knowing that Abdal and Selima must be exhausted. She had slept for several hours in the back of the car on their journey. They had stopped at a remote farm five miles from where the attack occurred. Selima had paused and spoken to the farmer while his wife ushered Aimee and Abdal into the house. Aimee had changed into the outfit that Abdal brought for her and emerged looking like a young boy instead of a woman. She had grinned at Abdal when he did a double-take and shook his head.

"The joys of being small," she had quipped.

The farmer's wife insisted on packing a bag of food for them before they departed. Selima told Aimee that the government would ensure the farmer was rewarded for lending them the horses and providing food and hospitality.

"We will reach the nearest location circled on the map within the hour," Selima said.

They were headed to a cave that was west of where the attack had taken place. Selima said it had already been searched, but perhaps they had missed something. This cave was on the map in Aimee's possession for a reason.

"I don't know why we didn't just report the information Aimee gave us. If we had, the entire Royal Military could be swarming these locations on the map," Abdal said.

"Surprise is on our side. We must use it to our advantage or Qadir will be dead before the cavalry gets to him," Selima stated.

The thought of Qadir being killed pierced Aimee with despair. They had to rescue him before Coldhouse or Andrius did any more harm. She looked out over the landscape. It was rugged and beautiful even at night—and vastly different from what she was used to.

She looked at the sky, and her breath caught. She had never seen so many stars. Heck, in New York, she had never seen stars at all! Out here, where there were no lights except for the glittering balls of gas above, she could see them all the way to the horizon.

"It is beautiful here," she murmured.

Selima reined her horse to a stop and dismounted. Aimee and Abdal followed suit. Selima motioned for Abdal to hold the reins of the horses. He took the leads and guided the horses off the trail.

"We will go on foot from here. I don't want to risk the horses alerting anyone. Do you know how to use a gun?" Selima asked.

Aimee looked at the weapon Selima was holding out to her. She nodded. She didn't like guns, but if it came down to their lives or Coldhouse's, she wouldn't hesitate to use one. She took the weapon, checked to make sure the safety was on, and tucked it into the waistband of her trousers.

Selima signaled Abdal to stay, and he nodded. If things went south, he would alert the Royal Military and convey their position.

Aimee and Selima covered nearly a mile at a fast pace before Selima stopped and signaled Aimee to be quiet. Selima pointed toward a cave and held out night vision goggles. Aimee nodded and took them.

They scanned the area, searching for any signs of life. After ten minutes, they cautiously moved in. Selima motioned that she would go first. Aimee swallowed and nodded when she saw the woman pull out her pistol. Aimee pressed herself against the uneven rock while Selima disappeared inside. Time slowed as she listened and waited.

"Clear," Selima called in a low voice.

Aimee relaxed and entered the cave. Three Humvees were parked inside along with a cache of equipment and weapons. Aimee trailed a finger along several dents caused by bullets.

"Why would they abandon their mode of transportation?" she asked.

Selima was still searching the vehicles. "It would have been too dangerous. Coldhouse's forces would probably have been seen by the military covering the main roads. Their best chance is to use the trails along the narrow passes."

Aimee pulled the map out of her pocket, spread it out on the hood of the first Humvee and shined a small, red penlight on it. She traced a path heading north from their position. There was a small village between their location and the circle near the border.

"How far ahead of us do you think they are?" she asked.

Selima studied the map. "Three, maybe four hours. They are traveling on foot, and they will be carrying some equipment—and have a prisoner," she said, holding up a black hood.

Aimee's blood ran cold at the sight of the material. She reached for it, touching a stiff spot that felt like dried blood.

"Do you think he's still alive?" she asked in a voice husky with emotion.

"Yes. I suspect they need him alive—at least until they get across the border. If we push the horses, we should be able to catch up with them by dawn," Selima said, taking the hood from Aimee's numb fingers.

"What happens when we do that?"

"If it is possible to make a safe extraction, we do so. If not, I will contact my superiors and advise them to send in a specialized team."

"Will they be able to get here in time?"

Selima smiled. "Yes, I've been in communication with them since the moment you arrived. They'll back us up when we confirm the targets and secure Qadir's safety as well as we can."

Aimee nodded and looked back at the map. They were so close and yet it felt as if they were a million miles away. She folded the map and slid it back into her pocket.

"We'd better get moving," Aimee murmured.

Seventeen

"I estimate about thirty-five villagers and ten hostiles," Abdal said, peering through the binoculars.

"The tall one to the left is Anderson Coldhouse," Aimee said.

"I count the same number. I don't see his brother," Selima commented.

The men had gathered the villagers in the center of the village. Women rocked crying babies and soothed the children while the men sat in silence, glaring at their captors. Aimee scanned the area for any sign of Qadir.

Selima pointed. "There. The house on the far left. There are two men standing guard in front of it," she murmured.

"We can't do anything while they have the villagers under guard. We don't want another massacre like that village to the east," Abdal replied.

A man standing next to Anderson began speaking to the group in Arabic. Aimee heard enough to get the gist of it—*'go about your daily lives, but don't try anything or else'*.

The group was slowly dispersing until two of Anderson's goons grabbed a man by the arms and held him back. The crowd stopped to protest, but the interpreter gave them a sharp order.

"He is the village Elder. They will hold him as a prisoner to keep the others under control," Selima said.

The Elder was forced into the guarded house. Aimee bit her lip and stared at the structure. She wished she had superpowers.

"I will go into the village and see if I can find out what is going on," Selima said.

Abdal frowned. "It is too dangerous," he hissed.

Selima lifted an eyebrow. "Do you want to go?" she asked.

Abdal grimaced and released her arm. "No… but, I will," he said.

Selima shook her head. "Stop thinking of me as your sister for a moment, Abdal. Those men will not see me as a threat. Most men, especially from the Western half of the world, have a preconceived notion that women are weak. I'll use that to my advantage. It is better if you two stay hidden until I return."

"I think it would be better if I went," Aimee said.

Selima looked at her and frowned. "It would be too dangerous," she said.

"Not if they think I'm just a boy with a ball," Aimee argued.

"I think you are both crazy," Abdal said.

"You wait here," Selima quietly ordered. "I'll scout the area. If something happens to me, you and Abdal will be the Sheikh's only hope," she said with a look that dared her to disagree.

Aimee sighed and reluctantly nodded. Selima was right. There was no sense in risking everyone.

SOMETHING ABOUT AIMEE

Selima slipped away from them. Aimee followed her to the outer edge of a sandstone house. Selima spoke with a woman sitting in the shade, then slipped into the woman's house and exited with a bucket.

Selima walked to the well in the center of the village, placed the pail beside the well, and lowered the bucket that was attached to the rope. She was in the process of pouring the water into the pail when the interpreter from earlier yelled at her. Aimee's breath caught in her throat. Selima carried her bucket of water over to the man.

There was an exchange of words, Selima looked like she was about to argue, but she picked up the bucket with a resigned, angry expression and disappeared inside the guarded house.

Less than five minutes later, Selima exited the house with an empty bucket and returned to the well. She refilled the pail with water and made it to the house where the woman lived unaccosted. Shortly after, Aimee saw Selima exit the building and retrace her path back to them.

The trio slipped into the shadow of a group of rocks where they could still see the village, yet remain hidden.

"Well?" Abdal impatiently said before she could.

Selima gave them a grim smile. "Sheikh Qadir is in the house with the guards along with the village Elder. He... has not been treated well. I overheard Anderson and the interpreter talking. The brothers were apparently separated by an unknown sniper. This third party caused the initial explosion that got our JRM's attention immediately, and the search for the Sheikh kept the brothers from meeting up along the way. Anderson is expecting Colin Coldhouse and a dozen more men to arrive sometime tomorrow," Selima said.

"A dozen!" Aimee responded with horror. "We have to get him out of there. How badly is he hurt? Can he move?"

Selima nodded. "I think he can. They want something from him and... I don't believe they plan on taking him out of the country," she said, touching Aimee's arm compassionately.

Aimee gazed back at Selima. She knew exactly what the woman was telling her. Colin Coldhouse and his brother planned on torturing the information they needed out of Qadir, and then they would kill him.

There was no way they could fight off two dozen men. Ten seemed impossible, especially when they were holding the villagers as hostages.

"We have to get the villagers to safety, rescue Qadir and the Elder, and disappear before Colin makes it here," Aimee said.

"I have an idea," Abdal piped up.

Aimee and Selima looked at the man in surprise. He shrugged and grinned. Selima waved an impatient hand at him.

"I play a lot of video games," he replied.

"And…," Selima said.

"Well, what if the villagers all disappear? I mean, they know this area better than anyone and can hide for months. I grew up in a village just like this. You tell one and they tell another and suddenly everyone disappears to their safe spot."

"Yes, but that still puts the odds at ten-to-three," Selima pointed out.

"We'll need a distraction," Aimee said.

"Maybe we can help," an unfamiliar American voice interjected, startling all three of them.

Aimee twisted around and stared at two people standing a few feet from them. The woman was tall and dressed like a Jawahir man. Her face was covered with cloth. Her eyes were hidden behind a pair of dark sunglasses. Only the smooth, husky sound of her voice distinguished her as a woman. Her companion was slightly taller, lean, and carried a deadly cache of weapons. His face was covered as well, and it was impossible to distinguish his features, but there was something eerily familiar about them both.

Selima trained her gun on the woman.

The woman paused before lifting her hand to her sunglasses. She removed them and casually looked at Selima.

"Who are you?" Abdal demanded.

"You can call me Dallas. This is... Hamlet," Dallas introduced.

"Greetings," Hamlet said.

"You're American," Selima stated, not lowering her weapon.

Dallas nodded and looked down at the village. "Yeah, I'm trying to clean up an American-made mess. Unless you plan on killing us as a distraction, I'd appreciate it if you'd aim that pistol somewhere else."

Selima lowered her weapon, but her eyes still showed her suspicions. "Are you CIA?" she inquired.

Dallas squatted down next to them. "Now, I can't admit to the U.S. government being involved in an international incident. Let's just say we are on the same side. Some people in the world don't think Andrius Bronislav should keep his power."

"How can you help us?" Aimee curiously asked.

Aimee kicked the tattered ball between her feet. It gave her an excuse to keep her head bowed. Out of her peripheral vision, she warily watched Abdal striking up conversations with members of the village. Each person cast a furtive glance at the armed men before they nodded. Slowly but surely, everyone began disappearing from the village.

Selima carried the bucket out of the house and over to the well again. She called out a sharp request for Aimee to get the food she had prepared for the Elder. Aimee picked up her ball and hurried to the house.

On the table was a small basket with stoneground flat bread, goat cheese, and dried fruit. She picked up the basket and exited the house.

When she was a few feet from the guarded house, she dropped the ball to the ground.

Keeping her head down, she moved the ball back and forth while Selima talked to the guards in Arabic. They frowned and shook their heads. Selima motioned to the bucket of water, the basket, and the door.

The guards balked.

Aimee was beginning to doubt their plan when the door suddenly opened. Through her eyelashes, Aimee recognized the interpreter from earlier.

"What's going on?" he asked.

The first guard shrugged. "This bitch has food and water she wants to deliver."

The interpreter asked Selima in Arabic to explain herself. Selima kept her eyes down and softly said that it was her responsibility to bring food and water to the Elder.

"Who is this?" he asked, indicating Aimee.

Selima reached out and slapped Aimee lightly on the back of the head. "This is my brother. He is still young. He has no manners. It is time he learned responsibility instead of playing with his ball all day."

Aimee stilled the ball with her foot and slumped her shoulders. The interpreter was silent and Aimee felt like his eyes were drilling through her disguise. He finally grunted and stepped aside.

"Put the water and food on the table and keep your eyes down," the man instructed.

"You think Anderson's going to feed them?" the second guard asked with disbelief.

"Fuck no. He'll probably eat it himself," the first guard snorted.

"Shut the fuck up and stay alert," the interpreter ordered.

"Yes, sir," the second guard muttered.

Aimee kicked the ball through the door and entered ahead of Selima. She took a few steps inside and the door closed behind them. A soft gurgling sound made her whirl back around. Aimee stared in wide-eyed shock as the interpreter slid down the closed door. He had a hand pressed to his slit throat.

Selima stepped away from the man, the knife in her hand dripping with his blood. Aimee shook herself out of her trance, placed the basket on the table, and retrieved the knife hidden under the food.

The house only had two rooms, the main area and another without a door. Through the opening, she could see an elderly man sitting on the floor.

She cautiously approached the room's entrance. Selima signaled her to stop. Aimee froze in place while Selima scanned the room.

"Help him while I make sure no one comes in," Selima ordered.

Aimee nodded. She hurried over to the old man and sliced through the ropes on his wrists and ankles. He reached out a shaking hand and touched her arm, then pointed behind her toward the corner.

"The prince," the old man murmured.

Aimee barely stifled her cry of horror when she saw Qadir sitting on the ground in the corner partially hidden by a stack of crates. He was bound and blinded by a hood.

She rushed over to him, sliding the blade between the plastic straps around his ankles. She slid her hands along his dirty trousers to his tethered wrists. They were raw and bloody from the thick plastic strap around them. His fingers curled.

"Qadir, I'm here. We are going to get you out of here," she breathed.

"Is he capable of walking?" Selima asked from the doorway, her attention still on the entrance.

Aimee looked up at the other woman and shook her head. "Not yet," she quietly replied.

She tried to be as careful and gentle as she could while cutting through the strap. It was so tight, she could barely squeeze the tip of the knife between his wrists. His hands fell limply to his sides once they were free and fresh blood oozed from the deep gashes in his skin.

She cut the rope holding the hood on and pulled it off his head. His eyes were closed. His face was badly bruised, his upper lip was split, and there were gashes on his right cheek and left temple. She tenderly caressed his bruised flesh, stroking his face with her thumbs.

"Here, give him water. It will help. Not too much at first," the elderly man instructed.

"*Ashkuruk*," Aimee replied, thanking the man for the cup and the damp cloth he held out.

She placed the cup against Qadir's cracked lips and murmured soft, encouraging words for him to take a drink. He moaned and tried to turn his head away until some of the cool, soothing liquid touched his parched tongue. He parted his lips.

A loud thud came from the house's door, causing Aimee to jump and Selima to twist around. Dallas was being true to her word. Shouts and the rat-a-tat-tat of automatic gunfire filled the air. Aimee jumped again when fingers wrapped around her wrist. Her gaze softened when she saw Qadir's dark eyes staring back at her.

"Am… I… dead?" he croaked out.

She laughed in relief and shook her head. "I don't think it would hurt so much if you were," she tenderly replied.

He swallowed with difficulty. Aimee placed the cup back against his lips with one hand and ran the damp cloth over his face with the other in the hope it would help revive him. He reached up and took the cup from her with a shaking hand, put it to his lips, and drained it.

"More," he demanded.

The elderly man reached for the cup and hurried into the other room where the pail of water was. Aimee gently cleaned the blood and dirt from his face. He drank the second cup of water before setting the empty cup on the ground beside him.

"Help me up," he ordered.

Aimee wrapped her arm around his waist while the elderly man took his other side. Fear poured through her when Qadir winced at the movement, turned deathly pale, and swayed before stiffening his spine. They kept their arms around him as he took a step forward.

"How many men are there?" he asked.

"There were ten. Selima killed one. Dallas and Hamlet are taking care of the rest," she said.

"How many are from our military?" he gritted out.

"Two units arriving asap," Selima replied.

They all heard the fast approaching helicopters. The sound traveled loud and clear through the house. Bullets pierced the door. Selima twisted and sank down against the thick mud walls. Aimee staggered sideways. The move sent Qadir off balance. He would have crashed to the floor if she had not wrapped her arms around him and pulled him back against the wall.

"Don't touch me!" he snarled.

Aimee stared up at him, startled. He pushed her arms down from around him. An eerie silence filled the house when the last of the reverberations of gunfire faded. She slowly stepped away from him, and he turned his back on her.

Tears pooled in her eyes and overflowed down her cheeks. She lifted her hand and wiped them away, but they kept falling. Outside, she heard Abdal's loud shout of triumph. Selima rolled the body of the interpreter out of the way and cautiously opened the door.

The bodies of the two guards littered the opening. In the square, sand wildly blew in all directions as members of the royal guard rappelled out of the helicopter hovering above the plaza. The moment their feet touched the ground, the helicopter flew off and was replaced by a second one with more men.

Aimee remained standing in the small room while the village Elder helped Qadir to the door. Selima looked at her, then at Qadir with a concerned expression. Two members of the Royal Guard rushed to help Qadir. Aimee slid down the wall, her stricken eyes following him as he was helped onto a stretcher and then airlifted. Tears blurred her vision, and she wiped them away with the back of her hand.

"Aimee?" Selima said in a soft, compassionate voice.

Aimee shook her head and turned her face away. He hadn't cared that she was still alive. He hadn't even said goodbye.

She buried her face against her knees and silently sobbed. She really did lose everything when the FBI took her identity. Now, not even the man she loved more than life itself cared that she was alive.

Eighteen

Aimee stared out the passenger side window of Abdal's car. She and Abdal had opted to retrace their journey. They returned the horses to the farmer and picked up Abdal's car.

Dallas and Hamlet had disappeared without a trace. Selima traveled back to the capital by helicopter so she could report to her superiors. There was a massive manhunt for Anderson Coldhouse. He was the only one to survive the shootout.

Abdal looked up as a helicopter flew overhead. "They are still looking for the others," he commented.

Aimee didn't bother to nod. Abdal sighed. She knew she was being rude, but she didn't feel like talking. Both Coldhouse brothers had escaped. That meant she would have to go back to her life of obscurity.

"How much farther 'til we get back to the capital?" she asked.

"Another hour," he replied.

Aimee nodded. Their trip back had taken longer than the trip there. Abdal had passed out from exhaustion once they reached the farmer's house and slept for almost forty-eight hours straight. Aimee had been very tempted to take his car. It was a shame that she didn't know how to drive.

Instead, she had helped the farmer's wife during the day and stared up at the stars at night. She had picked out a half-dozen of the brighter ones that she would like to visit. She wanted to be anywhere but here.

There was no news on how Qadir was doing. The farmer had no internet, and she had no phone. Even poor Abdal was having withdrawals by the time they left.

Aimee glanced through the dirty windshield and frowned when she saw the line of cars ahead of them on the highway. Abdal slowed to a crawl before stopping completely in the long line of traffic. She sat up, trying to see what the issue was.

"It looks like they are searching the cars," Abdal commented.

"What for? Do they do that often?" she asked.

Abdal shook his head. "No. It must be extra security precautions since the Coldhouse brothers and their men are still free."

She frowned. "Surely they wouldn't be stupid enough to come to the capital when they were so close to the border? That would be suicide. I imagine the royal family has enough security around them now that nobody could get within ten miles of them."

"I don't know. The line is moving fast. It shouldn't take us long, which is good. I need petrol soon," he said, looking at the gas gauge.

Aimee watched as the car in front of them was searched. She felt a little self-conscious about the fact that she had bathed and changed into her American clothes of torn jeans, an oversize green T-shirt with a polka-dot chicken on the front, and her scuffed ankle boots.

"*Tahiat sayidi,*" Abdal greeted the officer when it was their turn.

"Do you have IDs?" the man asked in Arabic.

"Yes." Abdal handed over his identification.

SOMETHING ABOUT AIMEE

Aimee looked down at her hands. She jumped when another officer knocked on the passenger window. She pressed the button.

"*Tahiaati lak,*" she greeted.

"I need to see your identification," the man stated in Arabic.

Aimee reached into her bag on the floor, pulled out her passport, and handed it to the man. He looked at the image, then her, and frowned. He stepped away from the car with it and spoke into the radio attached at his shoulder. She leaned forward but she couldn't hear what he was saying.

"That was a valid passport, wasn't it?" Abdal asked in English.

Aimee nodded. "It's the one I was given," she replied in the same language.

The officer stepped back to the car and returned her passport. She breathed a sigh of relief. She was putting it away when two other men dressed in military uniforms walked over to the car.

"Ms. Jones, I must ask that you exit the car and come with us," one of the men said in Arabic.

Aimee looked at them with a confused expression. "Is there a problem? I'm here legally," she said in the same language.

The man reached for the door. Abdal quickly unlocked it. Aimee shot him a nasty look.

"They have guns—lots of them. We don't. Go with them. I'll contact Selima and find out what is going on," Abdal muttered in English.

Aimee realized he was right. She swung her legs out and stood up, clutching her backpack to her chest. She silently followed the two men to a military style vehicle. Another officer pulled open the back door for her. Aimee paused a moment, looking back toward Abdal before she ducked inside.

The military officer who had requested that she exit the vehicle climbed in beside her. Nobody talked as the vehicle pulled away.

Aimee turned and looked behind her. The other three vehicles that had been blocking the road fell in behind them.

She slumped down in her seat, suddenly exhausted from the last week. She had barely eaten or slept, and the cool, dim interior, the silence, and that familiar, depressed apathy she had been carrying the last few years washed through her like molten lead. Leaning her head against the window, she closed her eyes.

Only for a few minutes, she promised herself.

"Why isn't she waking up?" a deep, rough voice demanded. "You said there was nothing wrong with her!"

"Sire, she is exhausted and has been through a lot. As have you. She will still be here after you have both gotten some badly needed sleep. Her vitals will be monitored for the next few hours as a precaution, as will yours when you go back to bed!"

Aimee frowned in her sleep. The first voice sounded as if the man had a sore throat. The second one sounded like Dr. Fuah. The thought of Qadir's personal physician made her shrink back toward the darkness. It was safe there. It felt as if she were among the stars.

The second time she woke it was dark. There was a heavy weight across her waist, holding her down. She was too tired to move it, so she didn't try. Sliding her hand down, she thought she felt an arm. She decided she must be dreaming. Not wanting to let the feeling go, she threaded her fingers through the imaginary hand and fell back asleep.

When she woke the third time, she realized two things: she was hungry and she needed to use the bathroom. Sliding out of the bed, she stopped when her toes sank into a plush carpet. A swift scan of the room told her she wasn't in a hotel—at least not any that she could afford.

The urgent pressure on her bladder forced her to make a beeline straight for the bathroom. Closing the door, she relieved herself, then decided to freshen up. She unwound her hair, grimacing at the grit still in it. It took her longer to shower than normal. The hot water and powerful jets felt good on her sore muscles. She had to wash her hair three times to get all the sand out.

She closed her eyes and tilted her head back, enjoying the feel of water on her skin. A frown puckered her brow as she tried to remember how she got here. Her last memory was closing her eyes in the military vehicle. After that, everything was a fuzzy blur of images and sounds. She wasn't sure what had been real or just a dream.

Her breath caught when a pair of hands slid along the wet skin of her hips. She opened her eyes and stared at the wall when a hard body pressed against her back. Her hands clenched against the wall.

"You had better be Qadir Saif-Ad-Din or I swear you'll be a dead man," she muttered, already imagining how she was going to get out of this situation.

"You had better not be a figment of my imagination, *'amirati alkhayalia*, or I will wish I was dead all over again," Qadir's rough voice murmured near her ear.

A choked sob caught in her throat, and she turned, burying her face against his bare chest. The dark, coarse hair on his chest teased her nose as she rubbed her face against him. She wrapped her arms around his waist. He winced when she squeezed him a little too hard.

"Careful, *habibi*. I'm still recuperating." He chuckled.

She loosened her grip immediately, sliding her hands down and cupping his buttocks instead. His low groan and hard shaft indicated that he was feeling good things at the moment. She stroked his ass, enjoying the way his muscles contracted when she caressed him.

"Hi," she whispered, looking up into his eyes.

He answered by capturing her lips in a passionate kiss that made the water raining down around them feel cool. She hungrily returned his kiss, devouring him like a dying woman drinking the elixir of life.

It wasn't until her tongue brushed across the wound on his lip that she ended the kiss. She caressed his cheek, pausing on the bruises and cuts. He let her explore him, avidly watching her expression.

"I was so afraid when I heard you were kidnapped," she murmured.

He held her tighter. "And you took it upon yourself to return from the dead and rescue me?"

She heard the hesitant note in his voice. She wrapped her arms around him and closed her eyes. He groaned and held her against him, resting his cheek on the top of her head.

"I guess I have some explaining to do," she finally said.

"Yes."

His short response made her heart clench. He turned off the shower, grabbed a towel, and handed it to her before taking a second one for himself. He stepped out of the shower.

A low purr of appreciation slipped from her at the sight of his bare ass. He glanced over his shoulder at her and flexed his butt cheeks. A delicate blush covered her cheeks.

"I missed you so much," she confessed.

"I will be in the other room," he replied.

Aimee bit her lip and watched him exit the bathroom. Fear gnawed at her that perhaps he didn't feel the same way about her as he had before. Three years was a long time—especially when you thought the person had died.

She dried herself and dressed in her clothes. Her nose wiggled when she noticed the chicken on the front of her shirt. A wry smile curved her lips as she pulled it on over her wet hair. She was feeling like a chicken at the moment.

∼

Qadir paced the length of his living room. The last five days had been brutal. His rescue was still a blur in his mind. Anderson had enjoyed using him as a punching bag during his short incarceration. Qadir had no doubt that he would be dead if it hadn't been for Aimee and her friend Habib.

During Selima Abd Wahhab's debriefing, she had explained how her cousin in the United States had asked Abdal for an unusual favor. Habib was not aware that Abdal worked for the Royal Intelligence Service or that Abdal was shaken enough to notify Selima who worked in the Jawahir Intelligence under Tarek.

Selima's immediate supervisor had decided that Selima and Abdal would intercept Aimee and discover how much information she had and whether it was viable. After speaking with her, they had determined that she was not working for Bronislav. She had come on her own.

Her confession to Habib about being placed in the Witness Protection program had been relayed to Abdal, then to Selima, Selima's supervisor, and finally to Qadir.

Aimee didn't reach out to me—for three years.

She'd been alive this whole time, and she'd stayed away from him. It was devastating and miraculous and agonizing. If she had loved him the way he loved her, she would have risked anything for them to be together. She should have known he would protect her.

He stopped pacing as the realization hit him that no, he couldn't protect her. He looked down at the damp bandages around his wrists. Coldhouse had murdered countless people and almost killed him and his brother even though they had multiple vehicles of trained security men. How could he have kept her safe when he couldn't even keep himself safe?

A shudder ran through him when he remembered the touch of Aimee's hand against his face. He had thought he was hallucinating or that Coldhouse was playing some cruel, vicious mind game. He had been half out of his mind with thirst and pain. The vision of her— He closed his eyes as another wave of bittersweet pain swept through him.

"Qadir."

He turned and faced her. She was standing at the entrance to the living room. Her long damp hair was unbound, and a wide-tooth comb was in her hand. Her expression was uncertain. She looked small and fragile in her tattered jeans and oversized t-shirt. He blinked and tilted his head, staring at her shirt.

"Is that a polka dotted chicken?" he asked.

She pulled the front of her shirt out and looked down at the chicken, which appeared to have a case of rainbow-colored chickenpox. A wry smile curved her lips, and she glanced impishly up at him.

"It's different," she said.

He chuckled. "You didn't cut your hair," he observed.

She lifted the long, heavy damp strands. "It's my superpower," she softly replied.

He held his hand out for the comb and motioned for her to sit on the ottoman. He sat down behind her on a chair and gently combed her hair. There was something soothing in the act, and they remained silent as he worked the tangles out.

"Tell me what happened," he finally requested.

Her shoulders lifted as she took a deep breath. She nervously wound her hands together before she began speaking. He listened to each word, savoring the sound of her lilting voice.

"After you dropped me off at Stanley's, I began going through the next week's deliveries. There was an envelope addressed to you. It had blood splattered on it. I knew I shouldn't have opened it—it was yours, but I opened it anyway. When I saw—the images—" Her breath shuddered at the memory.

He leaned forward and kissed her neck. She leaned back against him. He rubbed his cheek against hers and waited until she was ready.

"I took pictures of the photographs. I knew they were important and was afraid something might happen. There was a map, too. I took it and then I heard the front door's bell. I knew Stanley wasn't coming in because he was at an event for his grandson. No one else should have been there, and if they did come, they would have used the employee entrance."

"It was Coldhouse?" he asked.

"Yeah, Anderson. He was looking for the envelope. Hartley, the FBI agent in charge of my case, told me it must have been tracked to Stanley's. Anderson didn't see me, but I was filming him. His partner came in and he—he shot him. Anderson saw me when I tried to sneak out. I thought I had gotten away from him, but he—he came to the warehouse where I was—was living. There was another girl there. Her name was Kylie. She took my coat. I was talking to you when Anderson came in. He must have thought Kylie was me and killed her, then set the building on fire. I was able to escape out the back. There was no way I could go to the police by then. I knew Anderson would have labeled me a cop-killer and I wouldn't make it through the night if I went there. I hid in an alley until almost midnight, then made my way to the FBI building downtown. Before I knew what happened, I was placed in protective custody. No contact with anyone. Three months into it, one of the U.S. Marshals protecting me was murdered and another one seriously wounded. Somehow Coldhouse or Bronislav discovered I survived the warehouse fire Anderson set after he killed Kylie. He must have known I was still in the warehouse somewhere. Probably because Kylie was wearing my coat. Anyway, Hartley decided that I needed to be placed in the Witness Protection program. They faked my death again, gave me a new identity on the other side of the country, a career, and told me never to contact anyone from my past again if I cared about them because if the Coldhouse brothers or Bronislav found out I was alive, they would use them to get to me and then me to get to you," she said, bowing her head.

Qadir saw the tear that fell on the back of her hand before she wiped it away with her thumb. He gently turned her around to face him and caressed her cheek with his thumb. She had sacrificed so much to protect him, to save him and his people. The uncertainty in her eyes tore a hole through his heart.

He shook his head, and kissed her. She kissed him back, her hands lightly running along his arms to his shoulders. Her touch was featherlight but it did all kinds of crazy things to him.

"Touch me," he groaned, kissing her neck.

"I don't want to hurt you," she replied with a breathless laugh.

He grabbed one of her hands and placed it on his crotch. She cupped him through his loose trousers. He rubbed her hand against him.

"You have no idea how much pain I have been in for the last three years. A pain only you can heal," he said.

She caressed his smooth stomach before slipping her fingers under the waistband of his trousers. She turned her face to his and parted her lips. He greedily accepted her invitation. It had been too long since he'd held her in his arms.

Nineteen

Qadir held Aimee against his side, caressing her bare hip. She sighed and rolled into him, threading her fingers through the hair on his chest.

"What are you thinking?" he murmured.

"Just random thoughts," she said.

"Such as?"

Her fingers stilled. "I was remembering your reaction… a few days ago in the house… after— I didn't think you— that you didn't…." Her voice faded.

He closed his eyes at the memory. "I thought you were a hallucination. I feared my mind was cracking. How could you be there when I knew you were dead? I had read the autopsy report a hundred times."

She sighed again and rolled over. Looking up at his face, she caressed his bruised skin, running her fingers down to his chin. He kissed the tips of her fingers when she rested them on his lips.

"Why did you bring me here? You— Habib told me that your father has picked out a bride for you. I can't… I can't stay," she whispered.

He kissed her to silence the heartbreak in her voice.

"I thought I lost you once, Aimee. I won't lose you again—ever. You captured my heart that day in the Harris Building with your defiance, your bravery, and your sense of humor. Three years ago, I was going to ask you to marry me. I am asking you now. Will you be my wife?"

Her eyes glowed with love, and she smiled that huge, brilliant smile he had missed so much. She rolled on top of him, cupped his face between her hands and kissed him tenderly with a passion that woke his satiated body.

"You bet your ass I will," she murmured against his lips.

"That's a good thing considering we haven't been using any protection," he teased, cupping her breasts in his hands.

It was mid-afternoon when Qadir slipped out of the room where Aimee and his mother were chatting. He walked along the wide corridors, heading for his brother's living quarters. The guard at the door bowed and opened it for him.

"He is expecting you, sire," the guard said.

Qadir entered Tarek's vast rooms, raising an eyebrow when he noticed his brother was sitting at a table on the balcony with paperwork in front of him. Tarek still looked pale, and there were lines of pain etched around his mouth.

"Shouldn't you be resting? Dr. Fuah said the only reason he agreed to release you from the medical ward was because you promised to take it easy and follow directions."

Tarek scowled and waved a dismissive hand. "It's bad enough he has assigned me a babysitter. I can't even go relieve myself without the nurse following me into the bathroom to see if I have blood in my urine."

"And do you?" Qadir asked, pulling a chair out and sitting down.

"No," Tarek answered in a terse tone before he turned his attention to the nurse. "Get coffee for us."

Qadir watched with amusement as the nurse bowed and hurried to order the coffees. *He* certainly would not want to nurse his grouchy brother.

"Perhaps Kamil should have assigned you a more attractive nurse," he mused.

Tarek glared at him. "I don't need a nurse. What I want are the heads of Bronislav and the Coldhouse brothers."

"Killing yourself won't make it happen sooner and you won't be able to enjoy it when we do," he replied.

Tarek continued to glare at him before closing his eyes and taking deep calming breaths. Qadir watched the tension melt from his brother's body with relief.

"It wasn't your fault," Qadir said.

Tarek opened his mouth, closed it, and leaned back in his seat. The nurse returned and served their coffee before bowing and leaving the room. Qadir noted the two tablets next to Tarek's cup. Tarek picked them up and swallowed them.

"We lost eight good men," Tarek said, looking out over the garden.

"Yes. Father has met with each of their families," he quietly responded.

"You could have died," Tarek continued.

"And, so could you, but we didn't. None of us know when our time will come, Tarek. We can't stop all the evil in the world," he said.

"We can try," Tarek replied.

Qadir bowed his head. "We can try," he agreed.

"I didn't believe it at first when I read that Aimee was still alive—that she had come to save you."

Qadir followed his brother's gaze to their mother and Aimee walking in the garden below. Aimee's hair was in a long braid. The end fell just past her buttocks. She was dressed in a simple blue, long-sleeve dress with a pair of black leggings. She moved like a dancer, elegant and confident—almost as if she floated across the ground.

"I didn't believe it at first either," he confessed.

Tarek turned his sharp gaze back to him. "Have you told Father that you are going to marry her?"

Qadir picked up his coffee and took a sip before answering. "Not yet, but I will. My biggest concern is keeping her safe. Bronislav tried to have her killed a second time. She was placed in the Witness Protection Program after a Marshal was killed. It won't take long for Coldhouse to recognize her."

"I swear none of them will ever get near our family again," Tarek promised.

Qadir smiled but it didn't reach his eyes. "You aren't the only one who has made that promise. It is time to call in a few favors."

Tarek smiled. "I'm listening," he said.

Colin Coldhouse stood stiffly by the window waiting for Andrius Bronislav to finish his phone call. He had left his brother in Simdan, the country just north of Jawahir, with strict instructions to stay put. At this point, he wouldn't be at all surprised if Bronislav ordered a hit on both of them.

Andrius ended his call and motioned for Colin to sit down. Colin eyed the pristine antique Victorian chair before he took a seat. Andrius didn't offer him a drink—another bad sign. He noted the pinched lines around the billionaire's mouth.

"My assets have been frozen by three governments, and I have been advised not to travel at the moment… for my health," Andrius stated.

Colin wisely kept his thoughts to himself. Andrius's mansion on the outskirts of Moscow was beautiful—if you didn't mind the snow. It wasn't a *horrible* place to be trapped.

Andrius tapped the arm of his chair with his fingers and continued to stare at him with a brooding expression.

"You disappoint me, Colin," Andrius finally said. "I don't like to be disappointed."

"It won't happen again," Colin promised.

"What was your weakest link?" Andrius inquired.

Colin stiffened. How he answered the following questions would probably determine if he walked out of the house or was carried out.

"There were two: intel and personnel," he stated.

Andrius studied him. Colin kept his thoughts hidden behind a mask of calm.

"What are you going to do to compensate me for your failure?" Andrius asked.

"You hired Cold Methods Security for a job. It isn't finished."

Andrius's eyes narrowed. "No, it is not. The war between Jawahir and Simdan never materialized because a spy infiltrated your ranks and you were unable to stop one girl from turning evidence over to the American government. Fix this mess, Colin, or else."

"Yes, sir," Colin stiffly replied, rising to his feet.

"And Colin...," Andrius called before he could exit the room.

Colin looked over his shoulder. "Yes, sir," he said.

Andrius didn't look at him. "Deal with your brother. I will not tolerate his incompetence again."

"Yes, sir."

Colin left the house. He pulled his gloves on and walked to the Humvee waiting for him in the driveway. Snow crunched under his feet and clung to his hair and clothing. John, his second-in-command, opened the door for him, and he climbed in. Seconds later, his driver was pulling away from the mansion.

Colin stared out the window at the snow-covered fields. At least they had managed to get out of there alive. When he arrived, he figured he had a fifty-fifty chance. His phone vibrated, and he looked at the caller.

Pulling his glove off, he answered the call. "What have you found out?"

He grimaced as he listened to an employee relay the information he had requested. Seconds later, he disconnected the call and sat back in his seat.

It would appear the dead don't enjoy staying dead, he thought.

Perhaps there was a way to kill two birds with one stone. It was time his brother corrected his mistakes—and Colin corrected his own—once and for all.

After typing the number, he lifted his cell phone to his ear. Anderson answered on the second ring.

"What happened?" Anderson demanded.

Colin's hard, dark eyes glittered with malice. "I have a job for you," he said.

Twenty

Aimee was enchanted with Qadir's mother. The Queen of Jawahir reminded her of her adopted mom, Yolanda. She wasn't as eccentric, but her love for her sons, the people around her, and her view of the world despite the darkness in it shined through.

Ihab's apparent acceptance of Aimee was also difficult to resist. She appeared fascinated by Aimee's unconventional upbringing and appreciative that Aimee was a part of Qadir's life. Aimee smiled when Ihab linked arms with her as they walked along the path in the central garden.

"You are a remarkable woman, Aimee," Ihab was saying.

Aimee blushed. "Not really. All I need is love, food, and…"

Ihab studied her face and Aimee's blush deepened. She gave the older woman a crooked smile and bit her bottom lip. Ihab smiled back at her.

"I can understand why my son loves you," she said.

Aimee smiled. "I'm pretty crazy about him too," she confessed before her smile faded.

"What is it?" Ihab asked.

Aimee caught a movement out of the corner of her eye and looked up. Qadir and Tarek were having coffee on a large veranda. Memories of their night together made her body tingle. She turned her troubled gaze to Ihab.

"A… friend told me before I came that Qadir was to be married. How much trouble will he be in if—if he doesn't, you know, marry the woman chosen for him?"

Ihab squeezed her fingers. "Melik can be stubborn, but he is not blind. Both of us wish our sons to be happy. Qadir and Melik will work it out," she promised.

Aimee remained silent and looked back up at the veranda. Her eyes locked with Qadir's, and she smiled. Everything would be alright.

The next couple of weeks seemed to fly by. Qadir was busy. Every time she had asked if everything was alright, he kissed her and told her not to worry. She spent her days roaming the palace grounds. She had even gone to town with Abdal and met with Selima for lunch.

This morning, she was meeting Selima for coffee at a cute café close to the RIS building. She sat up, stretching her arms above her head and wiggling her fingers. A sexy groan was the only warning she got before strong arms wrapped around her and pushed her back down onto the pillows. She laughed and wrapped her arms around Qadir's neck, squealing when he nipped her neck.

"I don't want to explain to Selima—much less to your mom—how I got a hickey on my neck," she giggled.

"You are a dangerous woman who loves to torture me," he muttered.

She flipped their position and kissed his neck, enjoying the feel of her lips against his skin. "Yes, you are so deprived," she teased. "Maybe I should give you a hickey, instead. Make it all better."

Qadir gently flipped their position again so he was on top. "When and where are you seeing Selima?" he asked.

She sighed and played with his hair. It was tempting to release it from his hair tie. The problem was that if she did, not only would he be late, but so would she.

"Soon. We're going to Sin Kafih."

"Make sure that you have the guards with you. No more slipping out through the servant's entrance to meet up with Selima. I know you are used to looking after yourself, but you aren't alone anymore," he warned.

"Who ratted on me?" she giggled.

"Half the staff. They worry about you," he said, kissing her hard on the lips. "Be safe and text me when you get back."

She reluctantly loosened her hold on him, and he slipped out of her arms. He sighed when his cell phone vibrated. She sat up, not making it any easier for him. His hot gaze raked over her naked body, and she blew him a kiss. The look he gave her promised retribution later. Aimee's body immediately reacted. She softly moaned with frustration.

She rose from the bed, showered, and dressed in a silky long-sleeve lavender tunic that ended at mid-thigh with matching pants that felt almost like she wasn't wearing anything at all. She braided her long hair and left it hanging down her back. Grabbing a white scarf in case she needed it, she picked up the beaded handbag she had found during her last visit to the market and slipped on a pair of shoes.

She grinned at her reflection. Yesterday, she had dressed in her tattered jeans and T-shirt; today, she looked positively presentable. She remembered at the last minute to grab the cell phone that Qadir insisted she carry with her at all times when she wasn't in their living quarters and slipped it into the pocket of her trousers.

Minutes later, Abdal picked her up in his Camry. They were nestled between two large SUVs with tinted windows.

"Do you think this might be a little conspicuous?" Abdal joked.

"You think?" she laughed before she shook her head and waved a hand toward the black SUV in front of them. "Qadir won't take any chances after what happened to him and his brother."

"I can't stay the whole time. Selima said she can drop you off at the palace," he said.

"No problem. I can always get a lift with one of the bodyguards. They would probably prefer it," she said.

"What's on your agenda today?" he asked.

"Shopping. There's an event at an art gallery tonight. There are supposed to be a lot of important people there, including the Ambassadors to the United States and France. Qadir wants me to attend. I don't think my normal outfits would quite fit in with what everyone else will be wearing."

He glanced at her. "I'd have thought Qadir would have ordered you a ton of clothes from Paris, Milan, New York or someplace like that," he mused.

Aimee smoothed a wrinkle on her sleeve. "He tried. I told him that he would have to wear them because I wouldn't. Maybe once we are married, but until then, I buy my own stuff—well, except for the cell phone."

"You are one weird girl. I don't know anyone who would turn down free clothes. My sisters wouldn't, that's for sure."

Aimee laughed and changed the subject. She asked about Abdal's family and told him she had talked to Habib yesterday, who mentioned that he had been promoted to the assistant of the producer's assistant, then asked how Abdal's work was going.

The day passed quickly. Selima helped her find the perfect dress for the evening in a little shop tucked away down an alley. Aimee playfully teased her bodyguards when they insisted on searching the shop before she entered, but she also let them know she appreciated it.

Happy with her findings, she gathered her bags and slid out of Selima's car nearly six hours later. She waved to Selima and hurried up the steps. When Qadir's strong arms wrapped around her, she gasped. He kissed her until she was breathless. She laughed, surprised to see him so playful in front of the staff.

"Somebody missed me," she murmured.

"My father wishes to meet you," he said.

The smile on her lips faltered. He reached down and took the bags from her. The servant standing nearby stepped forward and took the bags from him. A flash of panic hit her when she realized that Qadir meant his father wanted to meet her now!

"I—okay," she said.

Qadir smoothed a wayward strand of hair behind her ear and cupped her face. "He can appear intimidating, but he isn't really that bad," he promised.

Aimee looked up and smiled at him. "I can do intimidating," she said confidently.

"He can be more traditional," he explained, guiding her up the stairs to the second level.

"Explain traditional," she said.

"Our family was originally from the western deserts. Many of us still live in the old way."

"The old way.... Why am I not getting the warm and fuzzies about the old way?" she asked.

"Sire, the King is ready," a servant stated.

Qadir cupped her cheeks and smiled at her.

"Just be yourself, and he will love you as much as I do," he promised.

"Kiss me," she demanded.

Qadir looked surprised, but he leaned close and captured her lips in a tender, passionate kiss. She held onto him for a fraction of a second longer, even when the servant cleared his throat, before sliding her arms down his chest and stepping back. She gave him a crooked smile.

"How do I look?" she asked.

Qadir studied her for several seconds before he replied with a smile, "Like you have been kissed."

"Good," she said with a smile of her own. "I'm ready now."

Qadir raised an eyebrow at the mischievous expression in Aimee's eyes. He wanted to escort her in—and would have, but his father had insisted that he wanted to meet Aimee alone. The request had surprised him at first, but after their talk this afternoon, he had reluctantly agreed. His father wanted a chance to see for himself—unfettered by his son's protectiveness—if Aimee would be a good match for him. He had told his father in no uncertain terms that she was—and that he had already asked her to marry him and that she had agreed.

Her fingers slipped through his when his father's secretary opened the door and announced her. Aimee lifted her chin and did what she did best—she entered the room like a train barreling down the tracks.

That is another thing that I love about her, he thought, staring at his father's stern face before the door closed behind her.

Twenty-One

Later that evening, after their date at the art event, Aimee stood on the veranda outside of Qadir's living quarters staring up at the sky. There weren't as many stars visible here as there had been out in the desert, but unlike that time she had wished she was anywhere but here, this time she was thinking about her meeting with Qadir's father.

The King had been very polite, asking her dozens of questions about Yolanda, her life growing up, how she had met Qadir, and what she thought of his country. She felt like she was being interviewed—in a good way. She had asked questions as well. Melik's answers had been filled with humor and love for not only his family, but for his country.

She turned when Qadir entered their room. She had already showered and changed. The dress she had worn tonight was perfect for the event. She had felt confident mingling with the affluent members of Jawahir society and representatives from different countries.

"I'm sorry that I was delayed," Qadir murmured as he kissed her cheek.

"I figured something must have come up," she replied.

"You were wonderful tonight."

She leaned back when he wrapped his arms around her. "Everyone was speculating if I was the mysterious princess you are supposed to be marrying," she softly responded.

"Let them speculate. They would be half right."

She chuckled. "Were you able to get everything done?"

"Enough for the day. I wanted to be with you. I missed holding you in my arms. I really don't know why you wear this hideous thing."

Aimee laughed when he slid his hands under the oversized t-shirt that she wore as a nightgown. She wore it because she knew he would remove it the first chance he got. She pushed him back into their bedroom, caught the French door with her foot, and closed it. By the time the door gently shut, she was standing nude in his arms.

"I think you are wearing too many clothes," she said, tugging his bow tie off and tossing it aside.

"I need a shower."

She slowly unbuttoned his shirt. "That sounds like fun," she murmured, turning her attention to his trousers as he shrugged off his shirt.

They almost made it to the shower—but the bed got in the way.

Two weeks later, Aimee was visiting the market again with Selima. She softly laughed as she listened to Selima bartering with a vendor for a scarf she had fallen in love with. Her phone vibrated, and she absently pulled it from her pocket and answered it without looking. The only one who ever called her was Qadir, Abdal, Habib, and Selima.

"Hello?" she answered, her voice laced with amusement.

"Didn't Agent Hartley warn you to never return to your past?" a deep voice asked.

Aimee stiffened at the voice she would never forget. "I could say the same to you, Anderson," she retorted, scanning the area.

"One by one, each of your friends will die, unless...."

"I'm listening, shithead," she coldly replied.

"Tsk-tsk. You are so predictable. Born on the street, live on the street, act like you're still part of the gang on the street. Too bad about your friends there," he said.

A chill ran through her. "What are you talking about?" she demanded, turning her back so Selima couldn't see her face.

"The Yangs were a nice couple, it's a shame about the robbery. I wonder who will be next? Stanley Becker? Polly? Eric? Even your friend Biggie and his dear old grandma aren't safe and who was that guy you liked—Habib? You never know when there could be an accident on the set," he said.

"You bastard! What do you want? Why are you doing this?"

"At first, it was all about the money. Now... now it's personal. You made me look bad and I don't like looking bad," Anderson replied in a menacing voice.

"You did this to yourself," she replied.

"If you don't want any more accidents, I suggest you do what I tell you. If you tell your boyfriend or the bitch behind you, everyone you've ever known will be dead."

Aimee's eyes widened. Anderson knew that Selima was behind her. That meant he had to be watching them. She slowly turned, scanning the area again.

"I'm listening," she replied.

"You need to dump your friend and your bodyguards. I don't care how you do it, but you have fifteen minutes to get to the central plaza. When you get there, wait for further instructions. If you are one minute late, I make a phone call and Stanley Becker will be dead within the hour; and before you think of calling or texting anyone, remember that I have this number, and I'm monitoring it."

Anderson disconnected the call.

Aimee stared at the cell phone. Her heart was pounding. She needed to warn Qadir. Her gaze flashed over the crowded market again. Her cell phone pinged. Horror and grief filled her when she saw the bloody bodies of Mr. and Mrs. Yang. Turning away, she closed her eyes and fought against the tears that burned them.

She had less than ten minutes to get to the central market. The glint of an ornate curved knife in a silver sheath caught her attention. She looked up at the vendor.

"Kam althaman?" How much? she asked.

The vender responded, and she gave him the cash, took the knife, and slid it into the waistband of her trousers under her tunic. She peered under her lashes at Selima who was still arguing with the vendor before casting a glance around for the two bodyguards that had been shadowing her.

She wandered to the next booth, picked a dress off the rack without looking and asked for a place to try it on. The woman smiled broadly at her and motioned for Aimee to follow her. She held up the dress so the guards understood what she was doing, and she hid her impatience as one guard peered behind the curtain to make sure it was empty before he nodded to her.

Aimee stepped behind a heavy curtain, hung the dress up on a rounded wooden pole, and muttered a silent plea for forgiveness to the shopkeeper, Selima, her bodyguards, and Qadir for what she was about to do.

Pulling the knife out, she cut a slit in the back of the heavy fabric wall of the stall and slipped out the back. In seconds, she was weaving her way through the throng of shoppers.

∽

"Qadir, you need to see this!" Tarek said in an urgent tone.

Qadir frowned and looked up from the report he was reading. He took the tablet from his brother's hand, read the messages, and paled.

"Where did you get this?" he demanded.

"I ordered Abdal to hack into Aimee's cell phone and monitor any unusual activity. I was worried that the Coldhouse brothers would discover Aimee's part in your rescue."

Qadir picked up his cell phone and dialed Aimee. The phone rang several times before going to the voicemail he had helped her set up. Fear knotted his stomach. He dialed Selima's number.

"She's gone," Selima said as a greeting.

"Anderson Coldhouse contacted her. He wants her to meet him at the central plaza in... five minutes," he said, glancing at the time stamp and then his watch as he and Tarek exited his office. They ran down the corridors.

"I'm on my way," Selima said.

"Coldhouse has threatened to kill friends of Aimee's, including you, if anyone follows her. Be advised that he probably isn't alone," he warned.

"Then I'll have to make sure that he doesn't see me coming," Selima grimly replied.

"We are on our way."

Tarek nodded. "I've already dispatched the team I had in the vicinity and alerted her bodyguards to the danger. I've also instructed Abdal to notify the FBI about the threat to the people in the States that Coldhouse mentioned."

Six black SUVs pulled up in front of the palace. A guard opened the door for them, and they entered. The vehicle pulled away the second the door closed.

Tarek looked at him. "You know, I should have insisted you stay here. It will be dangerous," he said, holding out a pistol.

Qadir took the pistol and checked it. "I won't hide in my own country —or sit and wait while my future wife is in danger."

Tarek bowed his head in agreement. "Neither would I. Abdal was able to get a lock on Coldhouse's signal. He won't expect us to be prepared. Take this," he said, holding out an ear microphone. "You'll be able to hear and respond to the team."

Qadir took the device and inserted it into his ear while he tracked Aimee's location using his cell phone. Aimee was at the central plaza. They wouldn't reach it for another six minutes. He knew all too well what could happen in that time.

"I have a visual on Aimee," Selima said.

"Coldhouse is contacting her again. I'm piggybacking you onto the call," Abdal said.

"I'm here," Aimee said in a breathless voice.

Cold, deadly rage filled Qadir when he heard Coldhouse's sadistic voice.

"Head east along Plaza Boulevard to the Saif River bridge. There will be a path that leads down. Follow it until you get under the bridge and stop. I'll contact you. You have ten minutes."

Coldhouse ended the call.

"There wasn't enough time to triangulate his position," Abdal said.

"I still have a visual," Selima stated.

"Don't lose her," Qadir ordered.

Tarek had already spoken quietly with the driver. The line of vehicles changed direction. Frustration seethed inside Qadir when he calculated their time of arrival. He and his brother looked at each other when they both realized they could get there faster on foot.

"Pull over," he ordered.

The driver pulled to the curb. Before they had completely stopped, Qadir, Tarek, and a handful of Royal Military personnel in street clothing were exiting the array of vehicles. They ran through the crowded streets.

Sweat ran down the collar of Qadir's shirt as the bright afternoon sun shone down on him. He slid down the railing of a set of stairs instead of fighting his way through the people heading up and down the stone staircase. People turned, some laughing, some shouting, and others taking pictures as the group of casually dressed men led by two well-dressed men in flowing white thobes and the traditional white ghutra rushed past them.

Qadir signaled Tarek and some of the military to take the left side while he and the rest took the right. He held his hand out as he crossed the busy four-lane road. Once on the other side, he looked at Aimee's position. She would be at the sidewalk that forked to a path under the bridge in another minute.

"Secure the area. Don't move in until I have Princess Aimee safe."

They bowed their heads before disappearing into the crowd.

He continued in a fast walk, taking a steadying breath. Dressed the way he was, he blended in with many other patrons walking along the sidewalk. He saw Aimee and changed direction so their paths would intersect.

He pulled an earpiece from his pocket. Fortunately, a crowd of tourists converged around them for a brief moment, concealing their interaction. He purposely bumped into her.

"Put this in your ear," he murmured.

She flashed him a startled look. The fear in her eyes turned to relief, and she gave him a brief nod. He passed the device into the palm of her hand. Aimee lifted her hand as if to push a strand of hair behind her ear.

"You are not alone," he murmured, stopping a short distance from where he had intercepted her.

He turned and watched as she continued toward the bridge.

"You know what's going on?" she asked.

"Yes. Tarek told Abdal to monitor your phone."

Her soft chuckle made him smile. "It's a good thing we weren't doing any sexting," she murmured.

"This line is being monitored as well," he cautioned.

"Well, damn."

He began following Aimee again. Selima threaded her arm through his so that it would look like they were a couple. Between the headscarf and sunglasses, it would be difficult to identify Selima. She held out a pair of sunglasses for him, and he took them.

"Aimee, whatever happens, do not let Coldhouse take you," Qadir warned.

"He threatened to kill more of my friends, Qadir," Aimee murmured in a strained voice. "The Yangs—"

"They are fine, Aimee," Tarek interrupted.

Qadir saw Aimee shake her head.

"I saw the pictures. Anderson said—"

"The images were fake. I asked the FBI to verify the information. After what happened with Coldhouse three years ago, the U.S. Department of Justice has been monitoring the NYPD to ensure they purge their department of rogue officers," Tarek reassured her.

"You're positive?" Aimee asked in a barely audible voice.

"Yes," Qadir said.

Aimee's sniff tore another hole in his heart. If it was the last thing he did, he would destroy Bronislav and the Coldhouse brothers.

"I'm almost there," she said.

"I'll be there with you. Draw him out, and we'll take care of the rest," he promised.

Selima's grasp on his arm slowed them down. He realized that in his desire to protect Aimee, he had tried to speed up. He kept his focus on her as she walked down the angled path that led under the bridge. Several groups of people milled around the popular boardwalk.

"There is a bench under the tree. We will watch her from there," Selima said.

Qadir nodded. They walked down to the bench and sat down. He scanned the waterway that led out to the Indian Ocean. Dozens of water crafts, from luxurious yachts to small pleasure crafts, dotted the inlet.

"Tarek, have you identified any hostiles on the water?" he asked.

"We are working on it," Tarek replied.

"Sire, incoming," Selima murmured.

Qadir's eyes narrowed on a high-powered dark red and black speed boat. "Tarek..." he said.

"I see it."

Aimee noticed the boat as well, and she backed up closer to the support wall. Two boys walked by, eyeing her and trying to talk to her. He heard her tell the boys that she was waiting for her husband. They shrugged and continued walking.

"Two men in the boat. I don't have a clear shot yet," Tarek murmured.

Qadir watched as the boat pulled up along the retaining wall. His focus was on the boat, and he almost missed the dark figure who dropped from the bridge structure above Aimee. Her startled gasp echoed in his ear as the man grabbed her, picked her up, and tossed her down into the boat before jumping into it himself.

Qadir was already on his feet running as the boat revved up and started to pull away. He calculated the movement of the boat and the distance. With a burst of speed, he took the leap.

His feet hit the deck of the boat, and he slammed into one of the men, knocking the man out of the boat and into the water as the driver sped up. He gripped the railing to keep from going over himself when the driver turned the wheel sharply and the boat's stern swung close to the concrete retaining wall.

The move probably saved his life. The bullet from the gun Anderson had aimed at him went wide. Aimee struggled against Anderson, twisting and bringing her knee up toward his groin. Her blow missed when the driver turned the wheel again, sending her sprawling.

The driver twisted in his seat and aimed his gun at Qadir, but his head suddenly snapped back from a bullet striking the center of his forehead. The driver's body slumped and his weight pressed the gearshift lever all the way forward. The boat careened wildly out of control before the driver fell out of his seat onto the floor of the boat.

"Qadir!" Aimee's terrified shout jerked his attention back to her.

She held a curved knife in her hand and was struggling with Anderson who was lying half on top of her, bending her back over the side of the boat. Qadir gave himself a push and lunged at Anderson, grabbing the man's arm and twisting him around to punch him.

Anderson locked arms with him, and they struggled. Aimee slashed with her knife, cutting a long, deep gash down Anderson's side. The man stumbled back, hatred blazing in his eyes as he grabbed his side and aimed his gun. Out of his peripheral vision, Qadir saw Aimee throw the knife. Anderson ducked.

"Time to go," Aimee shouted above the roar of the boat engine.

Qadir's eyes widened when he saw the boat heading for the retaining wall on the far side of the inlet. He grabbed her hand, pulling her up onto the stern, and they jumped.

Twenty-Two

Qadir lost his grip on Aimee when they hit the water. The river closed over their heads and his legs became tangled in his thobe. He yanked at his outer clothing, pulling it over his head and letting it float away. Clad in his elegant dress slacks and a white, long-sleeve shirt, he could move more easily.

He twisted around, urgently searching for Aimee. He saw a flash of royal blue. She was sinking to the bottom. He swam toward her, reaching for her extended hands.

She looked up at him when he wrapped his hand around her wrist. Suddenly, with a bright flash, an explosion sent a shockwave through the water, pushing them backwards. He kept a firm grip on her arm, afraid to let her go in case he was unable to find her again. Together, they swam to the surface.

Gasping for breath, he held her close as they watched the flames and a dark plume of smoke rise into the sky. Royal Marine Guard (RMG) boats surrounded the area, and Qadir could see more Guards along the seawall. They both twisted in the water when an RMG boat approached them and stopped. Qadir saw Tarek anxiously leaning over the side.

"Are you two alright?" Tarek called.

Qadir lifted his hand and raised his thumb. Tarek grinned and spoke to the officer navigating the boat. Seconds later, he was boosting Aimee up onto the ladder with Tarek's help. He climbed up after her, nodding his thanks to his brother. One of the two officers had wrapped an emergency blanket around Aimee and was guiding her to a seat in front of the center console.

"Anderson?" Qadir asked, his gaze on the scene near the retraining wall.

"We won't know until we search the wreckage and have the waterway dredged. I only saw you two go over the side. I won't be satisfied until I have Anderson's body."

"Find him. What about the man I knocked overboard?"

"We have him. I will interrogate him," Tarek assured him.

Qadir nodded. The officer tried to hand him an emergency blanket, and he waved it away. His concern was for Aimee. He skirted the center console to the boat's bow.

Aimee looked up at him and scooted over, giving him room to sit beside her. He sat on the edge and wrapped his arm around her. She rubbed her cheek against his shoulder.

"I lost my earpiece," she murmured.

He chuckled. "I lost mine as well. I'm sure Tarek has a whole box of them hidden in his office somewhere."

"I have to remember to thank him and Abdal for hacking my phone. I'm going to need a new one. I think I lost that, too," she said, feeling in her pocket.

He threaded his fingers through hers. "I'm not worried about earpieces or phones, just you, *habibi*," he murmured, kissing her temple.

"I wanted to tell you what was happening. I didn't have time or know how to," she said.

Qadir held her closer, feeling the trembling running through her body. Concerned that she might have been injured and not realize it because of shock, he called out for the officer to head to shore. An ambulance was waiting for them by the time they arrived.

He disembarked and held out his hand to Aimee. The moment she was on the concrete platform, he lifted her into his arms and carried her up the steps to the waiting medical personnel. She tried to protest, but he kissed her into silence.

"Do this for me," he said.

She sighed and laid back on the gurney. He held her hand while the medical attendant placed a blood pressure cuff around her arm. She closed her eyes. He squeezed her hand in concern.

"I'm okay. I'm just hiding my embarrassment," she informed him.

The attendant chuckled. "We'll transport her to the hospital. Would you like to ride with her, sire?" the woman asked.

"Yes," he said.

Thirty minutes later, he was pacing the private room set aside for the attending physicians outside of the emergency ward while Dr. Fuah attended to Aimee. He had taken a quick shower and changed into clothes brought to him on Tarek's orders. His brother had remained at the site where divers were searching for Anderson's body.

He turned when there was a brief knock and the door cracked open. Dr. Fuah smiled at him and stepped inside, closing the door behind him. The elderly physician motioned for him to have a seat at the table.

"How is she?" he anxiously inquired.

"She is fine. A few bruises that will heal. I do not believe I have ever met a woman who so frequently finds herself in so much trouble. I would blame *you*, sire, if not for the fact that she has told me this is pretty much normal activity for her." He chuckled.

Qadir sank down into his chair and relaxed. "It will not be the norm any longer. If I have to wrap her in silk and keep her tied to my bed, I'll make sure that she is safe."

Dr. Fuah chuckled again. "I've seen how well that has worked for you. I do think a quieter life would be best, especially in her condition," he mused.

Qadir frowned. "I thought you said she was fine. What's wrong? What condition?" he asked, his mind flashing through everything that had happened.

Dr. Fuah smiled. "I think her condition may have occurred during one of the moments you tried to tie her to your bed, sire. I would like to see her in a month. I've prescribed some prenatal vitamins for her, and I advise against any more action-packed adventures, norm or not. I imagine you'll have enough of those in a few years," he said, rising to his feet.

Qadir stood up, the word 'prenatal' playing like a broken record in his head. He gaped at his personal physician, still trying to wrap his head around what the good doctor was telling him.

"Are you saying that Aimee—that we—that she is pregnant?" he choked out.

Dr. Fuah bowed his head. "Yes. I had the test done as a standard precaution, and it came back positive. Congratulations, sire," he said.

Qadir stood frozen as Dr. Fuah took his leave. He gripped the table as a wave of dizziness swept over him. A child—he and Aimee were expecting a child! A deep laugh slipped from him, and his eyes glimmered with determination. There was no way his father could disagree with his proposal now. Aimee was expecting his heir—the heir to Jawahir. That overrode any political agreement.

∼

Later that evening, Qadir closed the door to their shared bedroom. She had finally fallen into an exhausted sleep. A quick look at the time told him it was nearly midnight.

Two guards stood at attention outside their living quarters. Additional guards patrolled the palace. Qadir continued down the corridor to the family living room. Tarek was waiting for him, along with their father. He greeted his father, then looked at Tarek's grim face.

"What did you find?" he asked.

"One dead—the driver of the boat. One we have in custody," Tarek replied.

"Anderson," he demanded.

"Escaped. I've ordered roadblocks on all city exits and a search of everyone who tries to get through," Melik stated.

"Do you think it is possible that he survived?"

Tarek pursed his lips. "There is a strong current in the inlet. It is possible his body was swept out to sea. I will assume he survived until I see his body."

Qadir walked across the room to the bar and poured himself a drink. He stared down at the dark amber liquid. Frustration gnawed at him, and he looked back at his brother and father.

"Post notices for all fishermen to be on the lookout and make sure all ships leaving the port have been thoroughly searched. Father, I need—"

"I've already authorized a red notice on Bronislav and the Coldhouse brothers. I've put Tarek in charge of finding the Coldhouse brothers. I will leave Bronislav for you. I will take care of the international fallout," Melik stated.

Qadir bowed his head in thanks. "*Shukran lak ya 'abi,*" *Thank you, father,* he replied. He returned his father's patient gaze. "Aimee is pregnant."

He hadn't intended to tell his father in quite that way.

"That is wonderful news, brother!"

Tarek hugged him tight, and Qadir grunted, his injuries smarting. He grinned anyway, lifted his glass, tapped it against Tarek's cup, and drained the contents. His eyes were still locked with his father's. A smile of satisfaction curved his father's lips.

"I will handle the broken marriage contract," Qadir began slowly, eyeing his father's expression hopefully.

Melik shook his head. "That might be difficult to do," he replied with an amused smile.

Anger and confusion flashed through Qadir. Anger won. After everything he and Aimee had been through, he would not lose her to some antiquated law demanding that Jawahir's King choose his heir's bride. He would leave Jawahir before he lost Aimee and their child.

"I will never accept another woman," he swore.

His father walked over to a small ornate wooden desk inlaid with a 24K gold family crest and picked up an envelope. He turned and held it out to Qadir.

"What is this?" he demanded, taking the envelope.

"The information on your bride that I received two months ago," his father said.

Qadir placed his glass on the bar. He opened the envelope, drawing out the pictures and paperwork. His breath caught when he saw dozens of photographs of Aimee. The time stamp on them showed they had been taken over the last four years. There were several photos of Aimee that he remembered seeing when he ordered her to be followed.

Confusion swept through him as he read the reports. The word CONFIDENTIAL in capital red letters and UNITED STATES MARSHAL'S SERVICE were stamped across the top. The reports contained everything that had happened to Aimee over the last three years.

"She was working as a stunt double on movies? No wonder she thought jumping off a speeding boat was a good idea," he mused with a shake of his head.

"That was her idea?" Tarek said with a raised eyebrow.

"Why do you have this?" he asked his father.

Melik sat down in the chair. "Did you think I couldn't see the change in you when you returned to Jawahir three years ago? I knew something happened. Tarek told me a little. The reports I requested told me more," he said.

Qadir sat down in the chair across from his father. He was mesmerized by the photos of Aimee. There was one in particular that held him spellbound—she was sitting by herself, her knees drawn up, her chin resting on them. She was staring out at the ocean. In one hand was a magazine with a full-page photo. The photo had been taken six months ago when he had opened a children's hospital in the Eastern province.

"How did you know she was still alive?" he asked, rubbing his thumb over the photo.

"I didn't until I saw that picture you're holding. Fate played a hand in my discovery. A young tech was hurrying by one day. The folder in his hand slipped and this photo fell out and landed at my feet. I remembered Aimee from the photos taken when you were together. I recognized her immediately and asked the young man where he got the picture. He explained that it was of an American girl who worked with his cousin. I called in a few favors and received this report a few days before you were kidnapped."

Qadir studied his father's face. "Why didn't you tell me?" he demanded in a hoarse voice.

Melik leaned forward. "I had to be sure first. A reporter overheard one of my conversations with my secretary about Aimee—though I did not name her. The next day, my secretary warned me that news reports were already being released about your upcoming marriage to a mysterious princess. I was planning on telling you about my findings when you returned from your trip."

"You're saying that you chose Aimee as Qadir's bride?" Tarek asked.

Melik nodded and leaned back in his seat. "Of course. I knew Qadir was in love—and the photo proved to me that this mysterious woman who saved his life not once, but twice, would be the perfect bride for a Jawahir prince," he said with a satisfied smile.

"Did Mother know?" Tarek asked.

Melik's deep laughter filled the room. "Who do you think told me about Aimee in the first place?"

Epilogue

A Week Later

Qadir turned from where he was talking with his brothers and Father in the family room when his mother and Aimee entered. His breath caught in his throat. Even Junayd and Jameel, who had not yet met Aimee, and Tarek were speechless.

Aimee looked like a royal princess from a fairy tale in the brilliant royal blue evening gown with crystal beads flowing down from the bodice and along the folds of the gown. The scooped neckline with a long scarf hanging over her right shoulder showed off a tantalizing view of her creamy breasts. The memory of them bare in his hands, his lips suckling on her rosy tips, caused him to shift uncomfortably.

He flushed when he caught his mother watching him with amusement. Aimee's long black hair was braided with tiny white flowers woven throughout. He itched to release the silky locks and wrap them around his body. His two youngest brothers eagerly stepped forward and greeted her, and he couldn't stop himself from growling under his breath.

"You'd better watch them. They may try to steal her from you," Tarek murmured with amusement.

"Never," Qadir replied.

Aimee's delighted laughter followed by his brothers' caught his attention, and he scowled. Junayd and Jameel were acting like two love-sick puppies. He turned when his father cleared his throat.

"She reminds me of your mother when I first saw her," Melik said.

"She is a very special woman," he replied.

Melik nodded. "She told me of her upbringing. It was… very unusual," he commented.

"I don't care about her upbringing. It made her who she is today. She's a warrior at heart," he replied.

"I can see why you are enchanted with her," his father reflected with a proud smile.

Qadir watched his father walk over to his mother. It was surprising—or perhaps he had just never noticed—how in love his parents were with each other. He wondered if he looked at Aimee the same way as his father looked at his mother. He hoped so, because Aimee deserved nothing less.

He walked over to Aimee and wrapped his arm around her waist. "Shall we go?" he asked.

Junayd laid a hand on his shoulder and leaned closer. "If Father insists you marry someone else, I'll be happy to console Aimee for you," he joked.

"And I'll be happy to slit your throat," he retorted.

"No threats of mutilation before dinner," his mother chided.

Aimee giggled. "I feel like I'm back home," she said.

Qadir held Aimee closer as she joked with his brothers and mother. It was impossible to miss his father silently watching the exchange with a pleased expression. Aimee sent his father a beaming smile that lit up the entire room.

The gala event was to celebrate the announcement of Qadir and Aimee's betrothal. Dignitaries from around the world had been invited for the event. Their wedding would take place soon. More security would be there to make sure nothing spoiled the festivities.

Tarek fell into step on his left while Junayd kept Aimee distracted to his right. The moment they entered the main ballroom, Jameel stepped forward, bowed, and begged Aimee for a dance before Qadir hogged her all night. He reluctantly released his grip as his twin brothers argued who should get the first dance.

"Have you discovered anything about Anderson?" he asked.

Tarek nodded. "An injured man was seen stumbling out of the Northern Territory near the border with Simdan. The farmer gave the man water and sent his son to notify the nearest outpost. The man disappeared before they arrived. It is suspected he made it over the border," Tarek replied.

Qadir flexed his fists. "I want them, Tarek," he growled.

"I'm following a lead," Tarek answered, sipping the drink he had plucked from the tray of a passing waiter. "How are things going with Bronislav?"

"His stocks have crashed, his business partners are fleeing, and there are only three of his bank accounts that we have not frozen—yet. He is no longer listed as a billionaire," Qadir replied with a smirk.

"Good," Tarek said, draining his glass and handing it to Qadir. "Now, if you will excuse me. I see someone I'd like to speak to."

Qadir frowned when he saw his brother heading for a tall woman with sun-kissed skin the color of mocha. He remembered the woman as a friend of Aimee's from the nightclub they had visited. She was the singer.

He gazed at Aimee. She was glowing and attracting the attention of far too many men in the room, in his opinion.

Placing his brother's empty glass on the tray of a passing server, he walked out onto the dance floor. Jameel and Junayd grinned at him and went off to find another target to torture. The music changed to a slower tune, and he held his arms out. Aimee flowed into them, and he pulled her close.

"I have a surprise gift for you," he murmured.

Aimee tilted her head back and laughed. "Like this isn't a big enough gift?" she asked with a wave of her hand.

He looked around. The room was filled with people he knew, but so far, he'd only spotted one person who Aimee knew, and he suspected she hadn't seen Idella yet. He was about to whisper his surprise to her when a voice yelled from across the room, drawing everyone's attention.

"Hey, Wheels!"

The chorus of voices were filled with a mixture of happiness, awe, and love. Aimee gaped in surprise and pulled out of Qadir's arms. Standing in a tight group at the entrance to the ballroom were her friends from her old neighborhood. Stanley spotted her first and made a beeline for her, followed swiftly by the others.

"Stanley? Mr. and Mrs. Yang?" she exclaimed in shock, before looking back at Qadir in disbelief. "You brought *Biggie* and his grandma over here?"

"I thought you would like to invite them to the wedding," he said.

She burst out laughing and nodded. "This is the best wedding present ever," she confessed, turning as Idella began to sing. Tears burned her eyes. "This is the absolute best."

Qadir twirled her on the dance floor one last time before they were mobbed by her friends. "Only the best for you, Aimee," he tenderly said.

For more of Aimee and Yolanda's story,
look for Yolanda's Ray of Sunshine.

Next in the series is Colours of the Soul !

Flip the page for a sneak peek.

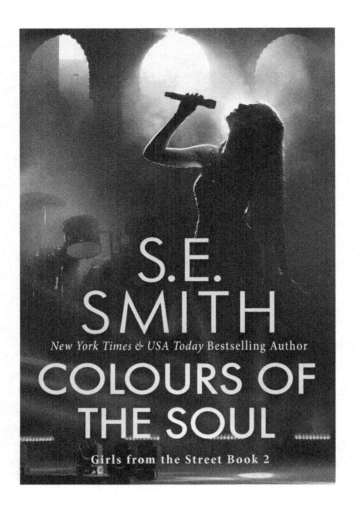

She was born on the streets; he was born to rule…

"We have to go. There is no time to save him," Raja impatiently said, pulling on her arm as he warily scanned the area around them.

"I have to stop the bleeding. He'll die if I don't," Dallas calmly retorted, laying her sniper rifle beside her on the dry, hard-packed sand and rock-strewn ground.

"Then he dies. The Royal Guards are dead. We will lose our targets in the mountains if we don't leave now!"

Dallas glanced up at the steep hill. Regret coursed through her. She had sent a message warning of the attack, but it arrived too late, and they had been too far away to reach the convoy before it started. The volley of gunfire had faded several minutes ago, leaving behind a desert painted in blood and filled with death.

She looked down at the barely conscious man. Determination filled her as she slid her sharp knife from the sheath at her waist. She knew who he was—Sheikh Tarek, the second son of King Melik and Queen Ihab Saif-Ad-Din of Jawahir. Their handlers would consider Tarek's death collateral damage. Even the capture of the Royal Heir, Sheikh Qadir, was not their concern. Raja and Dallas were here to eliminate Colin and Anderson Coldhouse.

Their objective was clear—and they were explicitly ordered to not deviate from it. Dallas knew she should leave Tarek to his fate, but she couldn't. She had met him before—in her life as Idella.

She turned to Raja with an impatient scowl. Orders be damned, she would do what she could to save Tarek.

"Get me the medical kit," she ordered in a tone that said she would tolerate no more arguments.

∼

Read Colours of the Soul

Girls from the Street Series

Novellas:
YOLANDA'S RAY OF SUNSHINE

Full-Length Books:
SOMETHING ABOUT AIMEE

COLOURS OF THE SOUL

MIDNIGHT SHADOWS

KATIE AND THE WARRIOR KING

THE GEEK AND THE SHEIKH

Additional Books

If you loved this story by me (S.E. Smith) please leave a review! You can discover additional books at: https://sesmithfl.com and https://sesmithya.com or find your favorite way to keep in touch here: https://sesmithfl.com/contact-me/ Be sure to sign up for my newsletter to hear about new releases!

Recommended Reading Order Lists:

https://sesmithfl.com/reading-list-by-events/

https://sesmithfl.com/reading-list-by-series/

The Series

Science Fiction / Romance

Dragon Lords of Valdier Series

It all started with a king who crashed on Earth, desperately hurt. He inadvertently discovered a species that would save his own.

Curizan Warrior Series

The Curizans have a secret, kept even from their closest allies, but even they are not immune to the draw of a little known species from an isolated planet called Earth.

Marastin Dow Warriors Series

The Marastin Dow are reviled and feared for their ruthlessness, but not all want to live a life of murder. Some wait for just the right time to escape....

Sarafin Warriors Series

A hilariously ridiculous human family who happen to be quite formidable... and a secret hidden on Earth. The origin of the Sarafin species is more than it seems. Those cat-shifting aliens won't know what hit them!

Dragonlings of Valdier Novellas

The Valdier, Sarafin, and Curizan Lords had children who just cannot stop getting into trouble! There is nothing as cute or funny as magical, shapeshifting kids, and nothing as heartwarming as family.

Cosmos' Gateway Series

Cosmos created a portal between his lab and the warriors of Prime. Discover new worlds, new species, and outrageous adventures as secrets are unravelled and bridges are crossed.

The Alliance Series

When Earth received its first visitors from space, the planet was thrown into a panicked chaos. The Trivators came to bring Earth into the Alliance of Star Systems, but now they must take control to prevent the humans from destroying themselves. No one was prepared for how the humans will affect the Trivators, though, starting with a family of three sisters....

Lords of Kassis Series

It began with a random abduction and a stowaway, and yet, somehow, the Kassisans knew the humans were coming long before now. The fate of more than one world hangs in the balance, and time is not always linear....

Zion Warriors Series

Time travel, epic heroics, and love beyond measure. Sci-fi adventures with heart and soul, laughter, and awe-inspiring discovery...

Paranormal / Fantasy / Romance

Magic, New Mexico Series

Within New Mexico is a small town named Magic, an... unusual town, to say the least. With no beginning and no end, spanning genres, authors, and universes, hilarity and drama combine to keep you on the edge of your seat!

Spirit Pass Series

There is a physical connection between two times. Follow the stories of those who travel back and forth. These westerns are as wild as they come!

Second Chance Series

Stand-alone worlds featuring a woman who remembers her own death. Fiery and mysterious, these books will steal your heart.

More Than Human Series

Long ago there was a war on Earth between shifters and humans. Humans lost, and today they know they will become extinct if something is not done….

The Fairy Tale Series

A twist on your favorite fairy tales!

A Seven Kingdoms Tale

Long ago, a strange entity came to the Seven Kingdoms to conquer and feed on their life force. It found a host, and she battled it within her body for centuries while destruction and devastation surrounded her. Our story begins when the end is near, and a portal is opened….

Epic Science Fiction / Action Adventure

Project Gliese 581G Series

An international team leave Earth to investigate a mysterious object in our solar system that was clearly made by <u>someone</u>, someone who isn't from Earth. Discover new worlds and conflicts in a sci-fi adventure sure to become your favorite!

New Adult / Young Adult

Breaking Free Series

A journey that will challenge everything she has ever believed about herself as danger reveals itself in sudden, heart-stopping moments.

The Dust Series

Fragments of a comet hit Earth, and Dust wakes to discover the world as he knew it is gone. It isn't the only thing that has changed, though, so has Dust…

About the Author

S.E. Smith is an *internationally acclaimed, New York Times* **and** *USA TODAY Bestselling* author of science fiction, romance, fantasy, paranormal, and contemporary works for adults, young adults, and children. She enjoys writing a wide variety of genres that pull her readers into worlds that take them away.

Made in United States
Orlando, FL
12 February 2023